A BLOW FOR LIBERTY

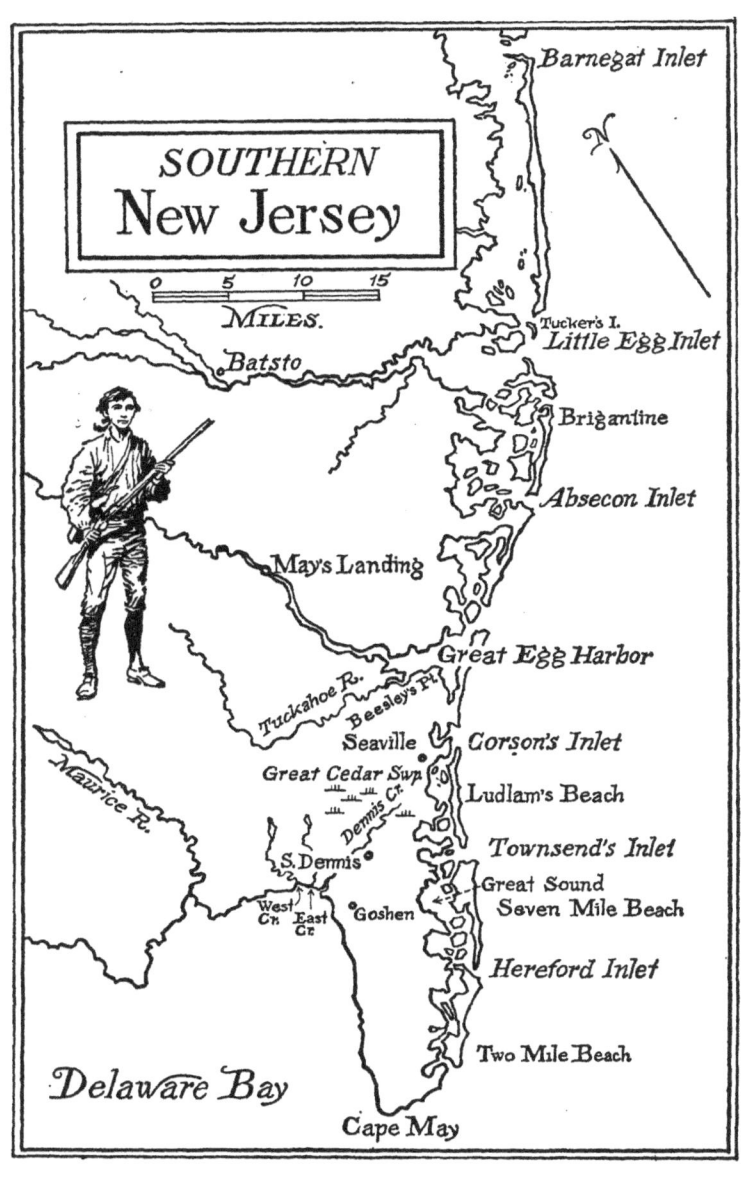

SOUTHERN
New Jersey

0 5 10 15
MILES.

Barnegat Inlet

Tucker's I.
Little Egg Inlet

Batsto

Brigantine

Absecon Inlet

May's Landing

Great Egg Harbor

Tuckahoe R.
Beesley's Pt.

Seaville

Corson's Inlet

Great Cedar Swp
Dennis Cr.

Ludlam's Beach

Townsend's Inlet

S. Dennis

Great Sound
Seven Mile Beach

Maurice R.

West Cr.
East Cr.
Goshen

Hereford Inlet

Two Mile Beach

Delaware Bay

Cape May

A Blow for Liberty

Stephen W. Meader

SOUTHERN SKIES

SOUTHERN SKIES

LITTLE ROCK, ARKANSAS

www.southernskies.com

Dedication

The republication of this book is dedicated with love to
James R.. West—musician, mentor, radio legend,
"America's Storyteller", and trusted friend
of 40 years— by Jerry Atchley

Foreword

I have never found Cape May County, New Jersey, mentioned in the history books of the American Revolution. Yet when I came here to live, I discovered that the county's people had valiantly borne their part in the struggle for independence.

No major battle was fought here. But out of a total population of only some two thousand, Cape May County sent hundreds of young men to fight in the Continental Line or in the four companies of militia raised here. More than that, each township had its group of Minute Men, ready to leave their jobs and defend their communities at a moment's notice. And nobody has ever accurately counted the number of Cape May men who built, sailed, and fought in the privateers.

My story deals with some of these patriots and how their efforts helped the cause of liberty. A few of the characters are based on actual people. All, I hope, are true to the spirit of the times and bear names that are still common in the county.

The Great Cedar Swamp, like the Pine Barrens to the north, was a favorite hiding place for gangs of outlaws called "Refugees," whose pretended loyalty to the British crown was actually a cloak for arson, robbery, and murder. The real Loyalists and Tories despised such men but were not above using them to spy on the patriots and pillage their homes. So it was that the Revolution brought bloodshed to Cape May County and to the bays and sounds and seas around it.

STEPHEN W. MEADER

7

A BLOW FOR LIBERTY

One

THE July morning was hot and still. Jed Starbuck could feel his clothes sticking to him as he crossed the yard to the barn, and he resolved that as soon as he was out of sight of the house, he would take off his linsey-woolsey shirt. Shadrach, the free Negro farmhand, was waiting for him at the barn door.

"Hot day, Marse Jed," he said with a chuckle. "On'y good thing about it, the wind's south. Time we gits to the water, it'll be a little cooler."

Jed nodded. "Let's be on our way, then. I'd like to get the wood loaded in time to catch the tide so we can save some rowing."

He led the way along the path that led southeastward through the cedars. At breakfast he had gotten his orders from Amos Townsend. The old Quaker had looked at him kindly over his square spectacles and urged him to finish his bacon and eggs.

"Dr. Harris will be needing more wood for the salt-works," he said. "I'm sending thee and Shadrach down. There's plenty of cordwood cut and stacked there by the landing, and I'd like thee to load all the barge will carry safely. If they have some salt made, thee can bring that back with thee."

The "plain language" of the Friends never sounded strange to Jed, for he had been raised a Quaker himself, back on the island of Nantucket. Now, as he swung along the trail with the sun beating on his bare chest, he thought about those long-ago days. Not all his memories of the island were pleasant. There was the constant summer wind, sighing above the beach plums and wild roses, the winter gales that rattled doors and windows, the mournful bleating of sheep, out on the Commons. And there were lonely women waiting for their husbands to come home from the sea. Jed's mother had been one of them.

He remembered her standing on the headland and shading her eyes as she looked for a sail, when he was a little boy. Nantucket ships had already begun making long voyages—hunting whales through all the seven seas. Sometimes they were gone for years. Sometimes they never returned.

Jed's father, the bearded Captain Elijah Starbuck, had come home on the fifth of March, 1773, and after the three years he had been away, his son didn't know him. Then, barely a week later, Jed's mother was taken suddenly ill with a fever. No medicine could save her. Jed remembered the bleak and windy day when they laid her to rest in the plain little graveyard.

That was five years ago. Since there were no relatives to take care of Jed, his father took him along as cabin boy on the next voyage of the whaler *Alice Brown*. She was small and old and leaky, and when they were six months out, somewhere north of Bermuda, a hurricane caught her and ripped out her mainmast. For three desperate days she drifted helplessly to leeward. Then, with the gale still blowing spray higher than the foreyard, her lookout sighted breakers ahead.

Captain Starbuck knew there was no hope for his vessel. He had the boats lowered and watched his son and the rest of the crew pulling shoreward while he stood alone on the afterdeck. Even as Jed watched, the bow of the *Alice Brown* struck a reef at the mouth of Delaware Bay, and a moment later she was gone.

Before they reached shore, the bigger of the two boats, with fourteen men aboard, swamped in the surf and sank.

Only six of the crew reached shore alive, among them Jed Starbuck, then a week short of his twelfth birthday.

Despite the heat, Jed shivered a little now as he thought of that day. He had sat in a corner, dazed and speechless, while the Cape May authorities debated what to do with this penniless orphan, washed up on their doorstep. The rest of the survivors had gone off to join other ships. There was no way to send Jed back to Nantucket and no family to look out for him there if he was returned. Finally they housed him in the county jail and put up a crudely lettered poster saying they had a boy for indenture.

Old Shadrach must have read Jed's thoughts. "Marse Jed," he said, "you's a mighty lucky boy. Ain't many boun' servants got as good a home as you. Ol' Marse Amos, he's a kind an' generous man. Treats you mos' as good as if you was his own kin."

"Ay, Shad," Jed answered bitterly. "But as you say, I'm still a 'bound boy.' If my father'd lived, I'd be at least a second mate by now. Or fighting for my country," he added with a note of wistfulness.

"Don' talk about fightin'," the gray-haired Negro told him. "You's a Quaker, like Marse Amos, ain't you?"

"Amos Townsend's a Friend," Jed replied, "but he's a patriot, too. If you talk that way, folks'll think he's a Tory."

"Hmm!" Shadrach grumbled. But he said no more, and they tramped on through the woods in silence. A deer went bounding lightly across the trail, and squirrels chattered in the oaks and pines. At last there was daylight ahead. They reached a rutted dirt road, crossed it, and plunged into another strip of woods.

"Gittin' close," Shadrach remarked. "Smell it?"

He was right. The salty, fishy tang of the tidal marsh was more noticeable with every step they took, and in a moment or two they came out of the woods at the edge of

Townsend's Sound. An area of blue water nearly a mile across lay there sparkling in the sun.

"Good," said Jed. "The tide's in, and we can go down on the ebb, after it turns. We'd best hurry, though, and get the wood loaded."

A broad-beamed scow, some twenty feet in length, lay tied to the rickety piling of a pier. The cordwood was stacked on higher ground among the trees and had to be carried from there to the boat. Jed rushed at the job like a colt taking a fence. He was a big, strong boy, tall, broadshouldered, and black-haired like all the Starbucks. He loaded his arms with half a dozen logs and hustled down the slope through the marsh grass. Out on the pier, he flung the load down, jumped into the barge, and began laying the wood in the bottom, stick by stick. To his impatient way of thinking, Shad seemed slow. But by the time he climbed out, the old Negro was there, carrying a still larger bundle of logs in his powerful arms. He let himself down into the boat, laid the wood on top of Jed's, and was ready to return for more almost as soon as his young companion.

"Slow an' easy does it." He chuckled. "Way you's tearin', you goin' be plumb tuckered out 'fore we starts."

Jed stopped hurrying and contented himself with keeping pace with Shadrach. After a dozen more trips, they had a full cord of pitch pine stacked in the barge. The sweat was dripping from both of them, and they paused a moment to rest.

A light breeze began to ripple the water. It was from the southeast, off the sea, and it felt cool and refreshing. They stretched their tired muscles, cast off the boat's mooring lines, and picked up the two clumsy oars. There was a single thwart, aft, on which they sat side by side. As they pulled in unison, the barge moved sluggishly out into the sound.

They rowed steadily and talked little. Shortly, they entered the mouth of a winding creek, where the ebb tide carried them along and they could rest on their oars. The creek widened after a while, made a big bend to the south, and swung down toward Townsend's Inlet. But the pair in the boat had no intention of being borne out through the rips to the sea. Instead, they pulled hard on their oars and crossed the hard-running tide, making for the inner shore of the long, sandy island known as Ludlam's Beach.

Close to the water stood a crude windmill, its arms turning creakily in the breeze, and it was toward this landmark that they steered.

"Can't pump much water till the wind freshens," Shadrach observed.

"True enough," said Jed. "And that lazy crew at the saltworks will just be sitting around, if I'm not mistaken."

They beached the barge and started toward the salt kettles, each carrying an armload of wood. Out of a shack beyond the windmill, a man appeared. He was well dressed, with a fawn waistcoat, neat white hose, and silver buckles on his shoes.

"Are you the men Mr. Townsend sent?" he asked. "I'm Dr. Harris, in charge here. Drop your wood by the fire, and I'll have my fellows bring up the rest."

He turned toward the shack. "Come here, you rascals!" he roared. "Monk—Eph—Johnny—come earn your pay!"

One by one, the crew shambled out, rubbing their eyes in the bright daylight. At Dr. Harris's command, they picked up a few sticks of cordwood and brought them to the hearth under the kettles, where a fire smoldered.

Jed was looking around with interest. The salt-making apparatus was simple. A pump, driven by the windmill, pulled sea water out of the bay to fill the pan. This was a foot-deep contraption of sheet iron, fifteen feet wide and nearly a hundred feet long. The sun evaporated much of the water in the pan, and when the residue was salty enough, it was run off into the huge iron kettles. Here,

over a hot fire, the rest of the water was boiled away, leaving a thick layer of grayish salt.

It wasn't a very efficient method, but with the usual supplies of salt cut off by the British blockade, the American colonies were desperate for the stuff. The going price of salt in Philadelphia went as high as seven English pounds per bushel—nearly seventy times what it had cost before the war. So a saltworks, even with lazy help, was sure to make a profit.

"We have some salt made," Dr. Harris told Jed. "Not much—only eight bushels—but it should be taken to the mainland for safekeeping. I've heard rumors there's a Tory ship on the way down here to destroy the works."

"Ay, sir," Jed replied with a tingle of excitement. "Our orders were to fetch back any salt you had. But about the Tories—do you feel safe here, or do you want some help from the Minute Men?"

"I fear we'll need any help we can get. Those Refugees are meaner than British regulars. The bloodthirsty devils don't take any prisoners." Harris dropped his voice to a whisper. "My workmen—if you can call them that—would leave in a minute if they heard about this."

Jed nodded. "Could you have them help us load the salt, sir?" he asked. "We'll get word to the soldiers at once."

Ten minutes later he and Shadrach were rowing homeward against the outgoing tide. It was a three-mile pull to the landing in Townsend's Sound, but they had a following breeze most of the way and were unloading the salt by noon. There was a big hollow oak tree in the woods close by. They packed the heavy bags inside the opening and covered them with brush so that they were well hidden. Then they crossed the road and hurried up the trail toward home.

At the farmhouse, Aunt Hitty, Shadrach's wife, had a good dinner waiting for them. But before he ate, Jed felt he should report to Amos Townsend. The old gentleman was sitting in his library. He heard the boy's story and looked grave.

"Dr. Harris isn't one to be hasty in his judgment," he said. "Thee'd better take a horse and ride over to Dennis Landing as soon as thee's eaten. Major Hand should be there, and thee can give him the message."

The old mare, Brownie, wasn't much of a riding horse, but it gave Jed a sense of responsibility to be using her on a mission of so much importance. He dug his heels into Brownie's fat flanks and shook her into an unwilling trot. The trail to South Dennis was used enough to be called almost a road. It ran fairly straight through a forest of pine and hardwood, bending only occasionally to avoid patches of boggy ground—arms of the Great Cedar Swamp that lay to the north. The middle of a hot July day was a poor time to see any wild game. The deer, Jed knew, were napping in shady thickets, and the night hunters, such as foxes and bobcats, were snug in their dens. He did hear the gobbling of wild turkeys in a beech clump south of the trail, but he caught no glimpse of the wily birds.

In less than an hour, he reached the first houses of a little settlement. South Dennis consisted of only half a dozen homes, strung out along the "Bay Road," which ran north toward towns on the Maurice and Cohansey Rivers. Jed's friends, Tom and Nancy Corson, lived there. He was tempted to stop, but his errand was too serious to waste time in visiting. He rode northward over a corduroyed causeway till the masts of sloops and schooners came into view above the trees, and he knew he was nearing Dennis Creek.

A boy about his own age was lolling on the stoop of a tiny general store. Jed pulled up and hailed him.

"Know where I might find Major Joshua Hand?" he asked.

18

The boy made no answer but grinned and jerked his thumb in the direction of Ludlam's Tavern, just beyond the bridge. Jed rode on, clop-clopping across the planks. In front of the inn he tied Brownie's reins to the hitching rail and went boldly up to the door. It was dark inside, and it took him a moment to adjust his eyes to the gloom. He could make out the sanded floor and the little bar at the back. And seated at a table near the only window, he saw a big, sandy-haired man in a deerskin hunting shirt. He knew that was the accepted uniform of the Jersey Minute Men, so he took a chance. "Major Hand?" he asked.

"That's right, boy," the man replied. "Who might you be?"

"Jed Starbuck, bound out to Squire Amos Townsend. He sent me over with a message for you."

"Very well, let's have it."

"Yes, sir. Dr. Harris, at the Townsend's Inlet saltworks, says there's a Tory ship headed down the coast. He thinks they're planning to attack him. If you can send some men, there's a boat to carry them at our landing."

The major nodded. "I heard the same report," he said, "from the Committee of Safety. All right, we'll be ready for 'em."

He rose, finished his noggin of ale, and strode to the door. Opening it, he bellowed a name. "Lieutenant Swain!"

"Ay, Major," came an answer from across the road.

"Lieutenant, mount at once and ride to Goshen and Middle Town. Pick a squad of eight or ten men and take 'em to Townsend's Inlet—the saltworks. Better see that they're armed and have provisions. You'll find a boat at Amos Townsend's landing."

"Right y'are, Major," came the reply, and a moment later Jed heard the pounding of hoofs on the road.

Major Hand turned back, pulling the belt around his

hunting shirt a notch tighter. He grinned at Jed. "The boys have been itching for a fight," he said. "Maybe they'll get one now."

He looked the youngster up and down. "By the way," he added, "ever think of joining up with the Minute Men?"

"I'd like it, sir," Jed answered. "But I'm not yet seventeen, and my indenture has more than four years to run."

"Oh, well"—the major chuckled—"this won't be a short war, I fear. You may still have your chance to strike a blow for liberty."

Two

THE sun was still high in the sky, and Jed was in no mood to hurry home. So, after bidding the officer a civil goodday, he strolled across the road in the direction of the docks that lined the creek bank below the bridge. There were several fishing boats tied up there, but more interesting to him was the activity at the shipways, farther down. As he drew nearer, he could hear the squeal of crosscut saws and the muffled pounding of mauls. More than a dozen men were hard at work on the skeleton of a good-sized vessel.

Since Dennis Creek was less than fifty yards wide, ships built there had to be launched sidewise, and the ways were set parallel to the bank. This method always astonished Jed, who had been raised close to deep water. Yet he knew the local shipwrights were famous for turning out staunch, seaworthy craft. One reason, he thought, was that plenty of good timber stood close by, and there was also a water-powered sawmill a short distance to the north.

As he stood there watching the oak planking being fitted to the ribs, he saw a young man he knew among the builders. Linus Jenkins was only a little older than himself, but he appeared to be doing a man's work, carrying timbers from the saw pit to the ways.

"What's she going to be, Linus?" Jed called out. "Looks like a big one."

Young Jenkins gave him a wink. "Pilot boat," he replied, chuckling. "Can't ye tell from her lines?"

Jed grinned back. "Ay." He nodded. "Biggest pilot boat ever sailed the bay, I reckon."

He estimated the ship's length at sixty feet and her beam at about twenty. She wouldn't draw very much water, though. Five or six feet would be his guess. In other words, she was much more likely to be intended for privateering. A ship that size, rigged as a two-masted schooner and mounting a few guns, could do some real damage to British merchantmen.

Jed had heard that there were already two or three such vessels sailing out of Dennis Creek. One had actually been a pilot boat in peacetime. Another was an oyster sloop, equipped with a small cannon. If they had captured any prizes, nobody had boasted of it, but this new ship looked more formidable. How he wished he could sail in her when the time came!

Regretfully he turned away, knowing he must start for home. Old Brownie still stood dozing in the sun before the inn, and Jed had to give her a slap on the rump to get her moving. Behind him, as he rode eastward, dark clouds rolled up to hide the setting sun. It was thundering when he reached the farmyard.

"Marse Jed," called Shadrach from the barn, "we-uns got to fetch up the cows 'fore it rains."

Cows! What a letdown from Minute Men and privateers! He unsaddled the old mare and called the dog. Trumpeter was his name—a big, rangy foxhound with a fine nose for trailing.

"Trump!" said Jed. "Go find the cows." And the hound was away like a black, tan, and white streak.

Like most of the local farmers, Amos Townsend had no fenced pasture for his cows. They were allowed to roam as they liked through the fields and woods. The young stock —heifers and steers—were taken over to Ludlam's Beach and left there all summer. To distinguish them from other owners' cattle, each animal had special earmarks, registered with the County Clerk. Jed knew the identifying marks well. All the Townsend cattle had a cropped right ear and a swallowtail fork cut in the left, and Jed had helped brand some of the calves in that way.

The air was heavy with the approaching storm as he and Shadrach followed the dog. Clouds of mosquitoes buzzed about their heads, and the old Negro grumbled as he slapped at them.

"On'y bad thing about livin' in Jersey," he said, "is them li'l bitin' bugs."

"You mean there aren't any skeeters in Virginia?"

"No, suh—not bad as these!"

"Well"—Jed laughed—"your hide'll get toughened up after a while. And anyhow, I guess you'd rather be a free man in Jersey than a slave anywhere else."

"Marse Jed," Shadrach replied soberly, "you done said a true word."

They heard Trumpeter's clear baying note beyond the next patch of woodland. Then, one by one, the cows began to appear, with the dog trotting at their heels. There should have been five, but Jed counted only four.

"Don't see Buttercup," he told his companion. "You reckon she's back somewhere in the swamp?"

"Could be," Shadrach answered. "She's due to have her calf any day, an' a cow gits notions, times like that."

The sky blackened, and a big drop of rain splashed on Jed's nose. "All we can do tonight," he said, "is get these critters in the barn an' milk 'em. Come on, you, Bess! Hup, Daisy! This rain'll be over by daylight, and we can go looking for Buttercup then."

Shadrach shook his head. "You do yo' own lookin', Marse Jed. I ain' settin' foot in that place. They's ha'nts in Great Cedar Swamp!"

Jed would have laughed at him, but the thunder was rolling louder and rain was pouring down in earnest. They got the cows under cover as fast as they could.

* * *

Amos Townsend was an early riser, and Jed wasn't surprised to find him at breakfast when he came down at five-thirty. In answer to the farmer's questions, he told of finding Major Hand and seeing the lieutenant ride off to gather a guard for the saltworks.

"And did thee come straight home after that?" asked the shrewd old Quaker.

"No, sir," said Jed with some apprehension. "I stopped by the landing to watch the shipbuilders at work."

"Oh, ay. That'd be Captain Dan'l Hand's new schooner. How's the work progressing?"

Jed was relieved. "They seem to have the ribs all in place, and they're planking her hull now. One man said she was a pilot boat."

Amos Townsend nodded, and his eyes twinkled. "Mayhap she will be, one day. But now for the day's business. I don't like to leave the salt where it is—too much of a temptation to thieves and renegades. So I want thee and Shadrach to bring it back here. You can take the red oxen and a drag."

Jed started to say something about the lost cow, but the farmer had already opened his big Bible. Each morning he read a chapter aloud before leaving the table, and it was no time to interrupt with worldly matters.

By seven-thirty the barn chores and the milking were done. Shadrach led out a pair of huge red oxen and yoked them, while Jed pulled the drag out of the shed. It was a toboggan-like contraption of heavy planks, used for hauling plows or other loads to distant fields. Back on Nantucket, Jed would have called it a stoneboat, but there were no stones to move here in sandy Cape May County.

They ran a strong chain from a ring at the nose of the drag to a ring in the middle of the ox yoke. Then Shadrach picked up his goad, took his place by the shoulder of the left, or "nigh" ox, and gently prodded the big beasts into motion.

Driving oxen was an art that Jed hadn't fully mastered. It was a painfully slow business, and he didn't have the needed patience. The best pace Shadrach could get out of the team was less than two miles an hour, and tired of walking so slowly, Jed went on ahead. Far behind him in the woods, he could hear the Negro's commands—"Hup, now, Rufus! Gee, there, Reuben!"

Later, when he reached the Shore Road, he heard other voices, coming from the direction of Townsend's Sound. After a little time, four men broke out of the woods, and when he saw they were carrying guns, he had a moment of fear. Then he saw the hunting-shirt costumes of the Minute Men and realized that he knew one or two of them.

"Hey, Jed," called Hiram Osborne. "You the feller that sent us on this wild-goose chase?"

"Why?" asked Jed. "Didn't the enemy show up?"

"Not a sign of 'em. An' worse'n that, Harris wouldn't let us in under cover. We had to sit out there on the dunes in the rain! It'll be a spell 'fore we come runnin' to save his stinkin' saltworks again!"

"Don't blame me," Jed told him with a grin. "I just carried out Mr. Townsend's orders. Here—I reckon you men must be hungry."

He had a canvas pouch slung over his shoulder with a lunch of bread and meat that Aunt Hitty had prepared. Now he held out some of the big, thick sandwiches to the Minute Men.

"Naw," said Osborne, "thankee just the same, but we brought our own rations. One thing I'll say—Harris was prob'ly right about the Tories. Just before dark, we sighted a big sloop offshore, hove-to outside the inlet. We'd built a smudge fire to keep off the skeeters, an' when her lookout saw all the smoke, she bore away to south'ard. Lieutenant Swain an' some o' the boys are still there, in case the sloop comes back. They say she's the *George*."

25

That name meant little to Jed then, but he was to know it better.

The soldiers departed, one going up the road, the others heading south toward their homes in Middle Township. Jed went to the hollow oak and began hauling out salt bags. Half an hour later, when Shadrach and the oxen came ambling into view, he had all eight bushels ready to put on the drag.

They worked at the loading together. Then, while the oxen rested and chewed their cuds, Jed went to the edge of the woods above the landing. He chose a pine tree that faced the sound and went up it like a squirrel. From a crotch fifty feet above the ground, he had an unobstructed view of the marsh, the creeks, and the open Atlantic beyond the dunes. He could see the windmill turning slowly and wisps of smoke rising from the kettle fires. It was too far to make out the figures of men, but the saltworks seemed to be carrying on as usual. More important, however, was the fact that not a single sail dotted the broad expanse of blue. The Tory sloop, if that was indeed the vessel Hiram Osborne reported sighting, had definitely taken herself off on some other errand. The only moving thing he saw was a fish hawk, sailing high in the sky.

He came down and returned to the drag. "I reckon they're all right, out there," he told Shadrach. "Everything's as usual and no ships in sight. Come on, let's have some food and get on home."

It was midafternoon when they reached the Townsend farm, unloaded the salt, and stored it in the toolshed for safekeeping. Then Jed went into the house to speak to his employer.

Amos Townsend laid down his quill pen and sat back in his armchair, looking at Jed over his glasses.

"Thee's brought home the salt?" he asked.

"Ay, sir. I saw four of the soldiers on their way home, and the saltworks are still safe. A sloop came close to the inlet last night, but I think they scared her off. The lieutenant and some of his men are staying on to keep guard. Now, sir, I hadn't a chance to tell thee, but one of the cows is missing. May I go find her?"

"Thee may. But thee'd better take the hound to trail her, and a gun might not be amiss. Aunt Hitty told me the cow is probably back in the Cedar Swamp, so thee'll get little help from Shadrach."

Jed kept a straight face. "I'll start right away, sir," he said and went to get his fowling piece. Outside, he started to whistle for the dog, but Trump had already seen the gun. He came tearing up to Jed, jumping and whimpering in his excitement.

"That'll do, boy," Jed told him sternly. "Just wait while I load, and we'll be on our way."

He had had plenty of experience with firearms, as any boy must who lived in sparsely settled country. Expertly he poured powder from the flask into the muzzle, rammed home a patch, then a load of buckshot, and a second patch to hold it in place. Last of all he put a few grains of powder in the pan for priming and checked to make sure the flint was properly adjusted on the hammer. Without such precautions his weapon was as likely as not to misfire.

Eagerly Trumpeter raced ahead across the fields, looking back to make sure he was going where Jed wanted. The nearest arm of the Great Cedar Swamp was hardly more than half a mile from the house, and it was in that direction that the boy headed. First he had to pass through open groves of oak, chestnut, beech, and other hardwoods. Then he came to lower, damper ground, where the cedars grew thick along a little stream.

The main part of the swamp was two or three miles across and nearly ten miles long, stretching across the county in a rough diagonal from northeast to southwest. It was a kind of no-man's-land, too wet and too densely forested to farm. The only visitors to this forbidding area were axmen after cedar for posts or shingles and hunters looking for deer or bear.

Jed wasn't afraid of the swamp, but he did feel a tingle of adventure as he stepped into its shadowy dimness. His feet squelched in mire, and he moved aside to a hummock of drier ground. Just then his eye fell on a footprint in the black mud. It was the track of a cow, sharp and unmistakable.

"Here, Trump," he called in a low voice, and after a moment the hound raced toward him. Jed knelt and pointed to the split hoofprint, and Trump's nose twitched eagerly as he sniffed it. Then he was off, not running but following the cow's scent at a businesslike trot. She had not taken a straight line but had wandered this way and that, getting ever farther into the swamp.

They must, Jed thought, have tracked her at least a mile when Trump came to a sudden halt. His hackles were up, and he was growling softly in his throat. Then a tall, slim figure stepped silently out from behind a tree, and Jed found himself looking into the black, expressionless eyes of an Indian.

Three

I T was only for a second that Jed was startled. Almost at once he remembered hearing about a lone Indian living in the Great Cedar Swamp—the last of the Kechemeches who had once made the Cape May peninsula their home.

Jed held up a hand in a token of friendship, and the tawny-skinned brave answered the gesture. He spoke with a guttural sound.

"Me Wagamissi," he said. "You hunt?"

"Just looking for a stray cow," Jed replied, trying to think how he might describe Buttercup in sign language. But the Indian appeared to understand.

"Me catch-um," he grunted, and turned to stride north-westward, deeper into the cedar thickets. Jed followed, admiring the noiseless way he moved. He was naked except for a deerskin loin-cloth and a pair of moccasins. Both sides of his head were shaved, leaving a roach of black hair in the middle. And into this scalp lock was thrust a turkey's wing feather. His skin was a kind of reddish saddle color, darker than a white man's but considerably lighter than old Shadrach's. Jed thought he was less than twenty years old, but for all his slender look, he was strongly muscled and moved with the quiet grace of a young stag.

Less than a quarter of a mile from the place where Jed had first seen him, Wagamissi halted, pointing ahead to a dense clump of young cedars. With Trump trotting ahead of him, Jed started eagerly for the covert. But suddenly the young brave lifted his hand in a warning. He motioned to Jed to get down, and together they crouched, listening. Puzzled, the hound turned back, saw them, and stayed where he was.

After a few seconds the white boy heard the sound that had already alerted the Indian. A stick crackled faintly. Then a low voice said something indistinguishable, and a second voice answered. Through the screen of brush, Jed caught a glimpse of two men, passing at a distance of sixty or seventy yards. They were headed on into the swamp, slouching along at a fairly rapid pace. One was tall and powerfully built, with stooping shoulders and gorilla-like arms. The smaller man had a long nose and a rat face and moved with nervous quickness.

Jed couldn't help shivering as he recognized the pair. The big one was Joe Crutcher, and his companion must be Al Jukes. Both had been in trouble with the law for years. Then, after the start of the war, they had dropped out of sight. Most people were sure they had joined the Tory cause and become "Refugees," like so many other unsavory characters. Loyalty to the king would have had nothing to do with it. All such men wanted was an excuse to loot and burn and rob.

Wagamissi waited until the two had gone out of sight and earshot. Then he stood up and spat, a look of disgust plainly written on his face.

"I know," Jed told him. "They're no good. You got any idea where they hide?"

But the Indian only shrugged his shoulders and stalked off. "Come," he grunted. And a minute later, in the middle of a cedar clump, he pointed triumphantly to the strayed cow. She stood there calmly, chewing her cud, and beside her, on uncertain legs, was a little spotted calf!

A grin of delight broke Wagamissi's stony reserve. Familiar as he must be with young fawns and other baby wild things, it was probably the first time he had ever seen a new-born calf.

"All right, Buttercup." Jed chuckled. "Let's see if we can get the two of you home."

Stooping, he picked up the infant calf in his arms and set off on the back trail. The cow followed close, nuzzling anxiously at her offspring. Then came Wagamissi, and Trump brought up the rear, ranging to right and left in search of woodland scents.

It seemed like a long way out of the swamp. The calf wasn't heavy, but it made an awkward armful, and once or twice the young brave took over the job while Jed rested. At last they reached the higher ground and more open forest. Wagamissi set the calf down, turned to the white boy, and made a gesture of farewell. This was as far as he wanted to come.

Jed watched his swinging stride for a moment. Then he vanished as suddenly and silently as a hunting cat.

The rest of the way home Jed's mind was on the two men he had seen in the swamp. Their presence so near the farm worried him. Of course, Cape May was a long way from the scene of heavy fighting, and after the battle of Monmouth that June, General Clinton seemed content to keep the British forces in New York. However, with so many of the local men away, serving in New Jersey regiments of the Continental Line, the Tories and Refugees were becoming bolder. Early that summer, barns had been burned—one in Tuckahoe and one in Fishing Creek. Both places belonged to families well known for their patriotic views, so there could be little doubt that the crimes were committed by renegade Loyalists.

Jed thought of the little bands of militia and Minute Men, scattered widely through the county, rushing here and there when danger threatened. What could they do if Refugees were to make a sudden attack on the Townsend farm, for instance? Then he remembered that the peaceful Quakers were rarely bothered by hotheads of either side. Probably his fears were groundless.

Perhaps, he thought, the war would soon be over, now that Benjamin Franklin had persuaded the French to help the colonies. But did he really want it to end? Somehow he would feel disgraced if the fighting was all over before he had a chance to be in it.

Despite his confusion of mind, Jed reached home well before darkness fell. He put Buttercup and her calf in a roomy box stall in the barn and went on into the house.

Aunt Hitty looked at him with disapproval. "Marse Amos done had his supper half an hour back," she told him. "What kep' you, boy?"

Jed laughed. "He won't mind my being late," he said, "when he sees what I brought home. Buttercup's got a pretty little heifer calf."

When he finished eating, he went, somewhat diffidently, to knock at the door of the study. Amos Townsend told him to come in, and Jed stood by the desk while the older man continued to study some sheets of figures. At last he laid them down and sat back, looking at the boy quizzically.

"Thy search seems to have taken thee quite a time," he said. "Did thee find the cow?"

"Ay, sir. She was deep in the swamp. Then her calf had to be carried all the way home. It's a heifer, sir, and a little beauty."

"That's good news." Amos Townsend nodded. "To tell the truth, I was a mite worried—thought something might have happened to thee. The swamp's a wild sort of place."

"I had a little help," Jed told him. "That young Indian, Wagamissi, knew where Buttercup was and helped me with the carrying. He seems friendly enough."

Jed paused and swallowed once or twice. "Another thing, sir. We saw two white men heading north through the swamp. I'm pretty certain they were Refugees—Al Jukes and Joe Crutcher."

The old farmer frowned at this news. "Hmm," he said.

"I hoped we'd seen the last of that pair. Thee couldn't have been mistaken?"

"No, sir. I had a good look at them, but they didn't see us."

"Going north, thee says? That could mean they were heading for the Tuckahoe River, or some of the settlements in Upper Township. Or it may be they have a hiding place somewhere in the swamp. Tomorrow I believe I'd best warn our neighbors up that way. We'll see them at Meeting."

Jed had almost forgotten that tomorrow would be Sunday—First Day, as the Quakers called it. That meant there would be no farm work except the milking and other necessary chores. And in connection with milking, he had better get out to the barn in a hurry and help Shadrach. After that he would have to take his weekly bath.

* * *

The morning dawned fair and bright, and a southeast breeze made it cooler than it had been the past few days.

With the barn work done and breakfast eaten, Jed went up to his little garret room and changed to his one good suit of clothes. He laid aside his cowhide boots and put on coarse white stockings and decent buckled shoes. His knee breeches were of gray homespun but clean and whole. And he had a white shirt, cut down from one of Amos Townsend's. With some care he clubbed his black hair into a knob behind and tied it with a length of narrow red ribbon.

The only looking glass in his room was a bit of broken mirror he had salvaged, but from what he could see of himself, he thought he looked well enough. He wished he had a three-cornered hat. The Quakers, however, frowned upon fancy clothing of any kind, and he had been given a plain round hat of rough grayish-brown felt.

When he came down, Amos Townsend was ready to

start. Shadrach led around the farmer's tall gray mare, saddled and with a blanket over her rump to accommodate Jed. Solemnly they mounted. Squire Townsend gathered up the reins and clucked.

"Get thee up, Jezebel," he urged the mare, and the gentle creature moved out of the yard at a trot. There was no conversation as they jogged up the Shore Road. After some three miles, they reached a little settlement that the local people called Seaville, and it was here that the Friends Meeting House stood.

It was a tiny structure, built of hand-hewn oak beams and native cedar siding. Already half a dozen horses and rigs stood under the trees in the yard, and Friends were greeting one another as they prepared to go in. Jed slipped down and tied Jezebel to the rail as her master dismounted. Amos Townsend moved ponderously to the steps, nodding to other members of the Meeting. He walked up the aisle and took his place on the facing bench that looked down on the congregation. Jed, meanwhile, had found an empty seat at the rear. The benches were hard and narrow, with very straight backs, but the young New Englander was used to such minor discomforts.

The last comers took their places, and the Meeting settled. There was a deep silence, broken only by the buzzing of a fly. The Friends sat in meditation for a long time, waiting for the voice of the Spirit to speak in their hearts. Nearly an hour passed, and Jed squirmed on his bench, trying to find a comfortable position. At last a small, frail woman rose on the right—the women's side. Her head was bowed, her white kerchief folded primly in front, and a dark gray bonnet covered her hair.

As she began to pray, her quavering voice filled the little room. She prayed for peace, that men might stop fighting and killing and that both sides might repent the sin of bloodshed. There was a saintly sincerity in her words that touched Jed, and yet he could not accept the

idea. To him, the American patriots were right, the British and the Tories wrong.

At the end of the prayer, there was more silence. And finally, when the children present were beginning to fidget, Amos Townsend turned to the Friend beside him and shook his hand. This was the signal for the Meeting to "break." Jed rose gratefully and grinned at a couple of youngsters his own age. Meeting was an ordeal he endured every week, but he was too staunch a Quaker not to know it did him good.

Four

Nobody was in a hurry to leave after Meeting. This was their one chance for social contacts, and for a quarter of an hour the women talked about babies, the men about crops and how the fish were running. At last the families bade each other good-by. Most of them rode northward, for they came from as far away as Beesley's Point. A large part of Upper Township had been settled by Quakers.

Amos Townsend and his bound boy climbed aboard the gray mare and started south. They had gone only a short distance and were just crossing the bridge at Ludlam's Run when Jed heard a distant pounding of hoofs. Amos Townsend pulled Jezebel over to the side of the road and waited till the rider approached. The horse was lathered and breathing hard, and the young man on his back looked haggard under a coating of dust.

He reined in sharply. "Can you tell me where I can find the nearest magistrate?" he panted.

"Thee's looking at one," the old Quaker replied with a twinkle. "I happen to be a Justice of the Peace for this end of Dennis Township. What might thy trouble be?"

The man coughed the dust out of his throat. "I've got a farm and a boat, up on Great Egg Harbor near the ferry," he said. "Last night some Refugees must have stole my boat. Anyhow, she was gone at daybreak, an' meantime Eben Davis's place, a mile further up, was raided. They run off six of his sheep an' burned a barnful o' hay. We want the law on 'em!"

"Yes"—Amos Townsend nodded—"I can see why thee's upset. But all this happened in Upper Township, out of

37

my jurisdiction. Even if thee reports it to the County Sheriff or the Militia, the men who did it will be hard to catch. With a boat, they could be a score of miles away by now. My best advice would be to ride back and organize the neighbors. At least a strong guard would prevent any more such outrages."

The horseman looked dejected. "Who'd be the magistrate in Upper Township?" he asked.

"Ephraim Jenkins is Justice of the Peace. But he's in Head-of-the-River, a dozen miles from where thee lives. I doubt if thy horse could hold up that far."

The young farmer agreed unhappily. "Reckon that's true. I sure would like to get those Refugee devils in the sights o' my gun. Well, I'll go home like you say, Squire, an' be ready for 'em."

Amos Townsend clucked sympathetically as the rider departed. "These are evil days." He sighed. "Wars breed wickedness as surely as rain breeds mosquitoes. I am a man of peace, as thee knows, Jed, but it is hard to think of turning the other cheek to such dastardly scum as these Refugees."

"I was thinking," said Jed, "that it might have been Jukes and Crutcher, up there at Great Egg Harbor. It's not much over a dozen miles from the swamp where I saw them to Beesley's Point. They could have made it with time to spare."

"Ay, it would be possible. But unfortunately they aren't the only renegades about. When good men go off to war, the bad ones come to the surface. If we didn't have enough of them here in the neighborhood, more are landed by Loyalist ships. As a practical man, I must confess that our privateers are a good defense against such marauders. Often they're a good investment for their owners, too."

Hidden behind the farmer's broad back, Jed indulged

38

in a grin at that last remark. As he well knew, most Quakers had an eye to profit as well as to moral principles.

"There's that new schooner that Cap'n Hand's building," he put in casually. "She's big enough to do well, if they fit her out for privateering."

"What does thee know about such matters?" asked Amos Townsend with asperity. "I think thee'll do better to put thy mind on the oatfield. The grain's ripe and ready for mowing, and thee and Shadrach will start on it tomorrow."

So, early next morning, the pair of them carried their scythes to the four-acre field where the oats nodded golden in the sun. Jed didn't mind mowing. The steady, rhythmical swing of the blade was a pleasure compared to the task of hoeing corn. It was good exercise, too, for his back, shoulders, and arms, all of which he secretly wanted to develop.

Around and around the field they went, keeping pace with each other. Once on each circuit they paused to catch their breath and whet their scythes. Gradually the day grew hotter.

Shadrach mopped his dripping forehead with a bandanna. "Why'n't you trot back to the house," he suggested, "an' fetch us a jug o' cold water? Gimme a chance to res' these ol' bones."

Jed had no objection to a break in the work. As he neared the yard, he saw Amos Townsend standing on the horse block, preparing to mount Jezebel. Knowing the farmer would question him about his absence from the field, he waited till the big gray and her rider trotted off. The direction they took, Jed noticed, was toward Dennis Landing, and that filled him with curiosity. It wasn't often that the Squire rode that way, for most of his business was at Middle Town, the county seat, seven or eight miles to the south.

39

He carried the water back to the field, and after a deep drink they started mowing again. By dinnertime that noon, Shadrach estimated they had cut an acre and a half.

"Be more'n half done, come evenin'," he told Jed encouragingly.

The scythe seemed to get heavier as the hours passed, but the old Negro never slackened the pace. By the time they finally started back to the house, there was only an acre of grain still standing in the middle of the field.

Amos Townsend was home for supper. After Jed had finished the chores, the farmer called him into his study.

"I'm going to tell thee something it would be better for nobody else to know," he began. "I'm trusting thee not to talk about it. Today I visited Daniel Hand and agreed to buy a half interest in his new schooner. There are risks connected with the venture, but on the other hand, the chance for profit is considerable. The ship will be called the *True Patriot*."

"Ay, sir?" said Jed, hopeful of hearing more, but his employer changed the subject.

"How did the morning's work go?" he asked.

"All down but about the last quarter," Jed told him. "Tomorrow I'll rake and pile it while Shad finishes up."

"Very good. And I'm sure thee understands why I'd rather keep my interest in the schooner a secret. Good night, Jedediah."

The fine weather held the next day, and Jed made good progress raking the oats into windrows and stacking them in neat piles. About two o'clock in the afternoon, he looked up to see a horse coming across the field. On its back rode a girl about Jed's age and a boy a year younger.

"Hello, Tom!" he called. "Afternoon, Nancy! What brings you over this way?"

They were the Corsons, from South Dennis, old friends of his.

"Ma promised us a blackberry pie if we'd pick the berries." Nancy laughed. "And Tom thinks the best place is up yonder at the edge of the swamp."

Shadrach laid down his scythe and shook his head. "Them young 'uns goin' git in trouble," he muttered darkly. "You better stop 'em, Marse Jed."

"Don't worry, Shad. The vines are thickest this side, where it's sunny and safe. I've got most o' my work done. I'll go show 'em the place to pick."

Nancy and Tom had jumped to the ground and tied the horse to a tree trunk. Each of them carried a basket, hand-woven out of the stiff bulrushes that grew in the salt marsh.

"Think we can fill these?" asked Tom.

"Maybe," Jed replied. "Anyhow, you'll have plenty for your pie. Come on—I'll show you."

He led the way across the pasture and right to the edge of the woods. There, among the stumps left from the clearing, was a vast tangle of blackberry vines, so dense that only rabbits and foxes could penetrate it. But all along the edges hung bunches of the shiny black fruit, ripe and sweet now in midsummer.

"You pick out here, Nancy," said Jed. "The brambles'd tear your skirt to bits if you went in. Tom an' I'll see if we can work our way inside. You willing to try, Tom?"

"O' course," replied the younger boy stoutly. "I've got my big knife to cut the stems if we get caught."

He had on knee breeches and hand-knitted stockings, while Jed wore boots and long dungarees. As a consequence, it was Tom who first yelled "Ouch!" when they encountered thorns. However, he whipped out his knife and freed himself, then started picking the big, juicy berries.

Nancy was making more headway than either of them. "Of course," she said, "if you want to show off, it's your

41

privilege to go in among those awful brambles. But I'm sure we can get all the blackberries we want right here along the edge."

Jed knelt to disentangle his leg from a particularly vicious vine. "All right," he said with a laugh. "I guess you're right. I surrender."

He fought his way out and dropped a handful of fruit into Nancy's basket. Tom, more stubborn about it, continued to flounder among the barbed runners and spent more time freeing his clothes than gathering berries.

"We're going to have a session of school," said Nancy. "There's a new Baptist minister, down from Cumberland County, who's been preaching around in different homes. When he heard we didn't have any regular school, he offered to teach the South Dennis boys and girls for a month. He doesn't make any charge except his board and room, and my folks invited him to stay with us."

She had poured all this out so rapidly that she was out of breath.

"Wish I could get a little schooling," said Jed wistfully. "I did go a couple of terms in Nantucket, but that was when I was pretty small."

"That's one reason I wanted to come over here for berries," Nancy replied, her cheeks coloring. "Don't you suppose old Amos would let you come to school? You could eat with us and sleep in the barn. You *will* ask him, won't you, Jed?"

"I don't know. Did you say anything to your father about it?"

"Only to Ma, and she's in favor of it. If she says you can come, it'll be all right with my father."

He picked in silence for a while, then asked her when the school would start.

"Next week," she told him. "Eight o'clock Monday morning."

"All right," said Jed. "I'll try. But right now I've got to

go back and help Shadrach with the oats. I hope the pie's good!"

"I'll save a piece for you!" she called after him.

* * *

Jed was unable to muster enough courage to speak to Amos Townsend until the next morning. After the Scripture reading he followed the farmer out to the doorstep.

"I was wondering," he began, "if thee would object to my getting a little more schooling. It'd only be for a month—over at South Dennis—and it wouldn't cost anything. They've invited me to stay at the Corsons'."

The squire frowned. "Thee can write thy name, can't thee? And read a little, and add simple figures? What more does thee need?"

"I'd like to be able to read real books—the Bible, for instance. Then it would be a help if I could do more with figures. Thee knows I never got past short division back home."

"Well," the old Quaker said, scratching his chin, "it might be worthwhile if thee had a bit more education. Thee'd be more valuable to me, I mean. And as soon as the oats are in the barn, there won't be any big farm jobs for a few weeks. When does this school start?"

"Next Second Day. I'll come home Seventh Day evening and go to Meeting with thee every week."

"Very well, Jed. I'll give thee a little money for books. Thee says thy board is free?"

"Ay, sir. But I'll try to be enough help to earn my keep while I'm at the Corsons'."

The weather was good to farmers that week. Jed and Shadrach hauled the oats to the barn without getting the crop wet. The threshing out of the grain could wait for another month or two. Meanwhile, Aunt Hitty was busy mending old shirts and breeches and darning stockings for Jed to take with him. There was no thought of his wearing his best clothes. Those were sacred to First Day Meeting.

They heard no more news of Tory depredations, and Jed's worries began to subside. He had wondered, at first, whether he should go off and leave the farm unprotected. If it were to become generally known that Amos Townsend was part owner of a privateer, the Loyalists and Refugees might take revenge. But as far as he could tell, the fact was still a secret.

On First Day he rode to Meeting as usual behind the prosperous squire, and his employer sat on the facing bench, nodding approval when someone rose to speak on the evils of war. Jed smiled inwardly. He knew most Friends were sincere pacifists, but he wondered how far Amos Townsend would agree with them if it affected his pocketbook.

That evening when the chores were done, Jed packed his belongings into a canvas sack. There was still an hour of daylight. He said good-by to Squire Townsend, Aunt Hitty, and Shadrach and set out to trudge the five miles to South Dennis.

Five

I T was a fine night for walking. Jed had his bundle of clothes slung on a stick over his shoulder, and it weighed little. He stepped out at a good brisk pace, putting as much distance as possible behind him while there was still daylight. Even after that, he had no trouble finding the way. The afterglow hung pink in the sky, and he made over half the distance before it faded to gray.

Then came a time of uncertain twilight, when the trail itself lay plunged in darkness, and only the treetops stood out in silhouette. The night animals began to come out. He heard faint rustlings and cracklings in the woods on either side. An owl hooted, startlingly loud. Jed hurried his footsteps and stumbled over a root, barking his shin. Fortunately his sack was well tied, and his belongings didn't spill out.

He picked himself up, angry at his clumsiness, and went on more carefully. After perhaps ten minutes of slower progress, he heard a brushing of leaves and suddenly a big black shadow moved across the trail a few yards ahead. He was pretty certain it was a bear, but he refused to be frightened. Boldly he marched on, stamping his feet as he went, and whatever the animal was, it went crashing off into the woods in panic.

Jed had no way of telling the time, but he thought it must be close to ten o'clock when he emerged from the forest and saw the dark shapes of houses ahead. Everybody in South Dennis had gone to bed, and not a flicker of light showed in any of the windows. He went cautiously through the gate at the Corson place, picking his way so as

45

not to make any noise. As he neared the barn, a dog began barking furiously, one or two houses away. Then a window was opened with a squealing sound, and a distant voice shouted a challenge into the night.

"Who's there?" the householder bellowed. "Clear out o' here or I'll shoot ye dead!"

Silently Jed found the staple that held the small door of the barn. He lifted the latch and pulled it gently open, trying to avoid any creak of hinges. He had been in the barn before, with young Tom Corson, so he had a fair idea where things were, and he crossed the floor, step by careful step. At last he found what he wanted—a pile of loose hay at the foot of the mow.

Gratefully he laid down his bundle, pulled off his boots, and lay down in the hay. It smelled fresh and sweet, of red clover and timothy. In three minutes Jed was fast asleep.

* * *

A rooster crowed loudly at dawn. Then the Corsons' horse lumbered to his feet in the stall and snorted, blowing chaff around the manger, hopeful of finding a few grains of feed he might have missed the night before.

Jed woke up, rubbed his eyes, and stretched. Getting into his boots, he went out to the pump in the yard and washed his face, neck, and arms. The sun was just coming over the woods to the east.

Looking about for something to do, he pitched down some hay for the horse, then saw the red and white cow standing in the yard by the barn, waiting to be milked. He found the milking stool and, afterward, the pail, hanging on a peg. Just as he was stripping the last drops into the full bucket, the kitchen door was flung open and out came Tom Corson.

"Good morning!" Jed called over his shoulder. "I'm your new stable boy."

"Well, for heaven's sakes! When'd you get here, Jed?"

"After you were all asleep. Thought I'd wake the whole neighborhood before I got bedded down in the barn."

"You mean you walked all the way over here in the dark?"

"Just the last part. Ran across something I figured was a bear, but he was a lot scareder'n I was."

"Well, thanks for doing the milking. Ma'll have breakfast on the table pretty quick."

The milk was carried to the springhouse to cool, and the two boys went into the big kitchen. Busy as she was, Mrs. Corson took time to greet Jed cordially and show him where he would sit. Before him he saw a huge platter of fried eggs, another of ham, and a basketful of smoking hot biscuits. Soon Samuel Corson arrived, and after him two younger children, a little boy and girl. Nancy was the next to come down, her cheeks flushing when she saw Jed at the table. And last of all the minister, who was to be their teacher, appeared.

The Reverend Peter Groom was a thin young man with fair hair and intelligent gray eyes. He greeted them all with nervous stiffness, then took his place and plunged into a long, fervent grace. Jed, used to Quaker silence, endured it to the end, but he was growing hungrier by the moment. Both boys were relieved when at last they were free to help themselves.

As soon as breakfast was over, Samuel Corson went off to his work. He was foreman in charge of the ship being built at Dennis Landing. By eight o'clock four or five of the neighbors' children arrived, scrubbed and ready for school.

Their classes were to be held in the Corson parlor. All available chairs had been placed in rows, and the Reverend Groom sat behind a small table, facing them.

When all were gathered, he eyed the children solemnly.

47

"We shall open by reading from the Book of Job, the thirty-eighth chapter," he announced. " 'Then the Lord answered Job out of the whirlwind and said . . .' "

He read the long, dramatic passage with feeling, his deep voice ringing out the words like rolling thunder. When he closed the book, all of them sat in awed silence.

"Now," he said briskly, "we'll begin our lessons."

The eight youngsters in the room ranged in age from a four-year-old to Nancy and Jed, who were sixteen. Yet the teacher handled his instruction with firm efficiency. He set the little tots to learning the alphabet, handed reading books to the next older group, and started the teen-age pupils on an arithmetic lesson. One thing that helped was that every one of them wanted to learn. School was a rare privilege, to be made the most of, and they worked hard.

Jed was behind the others in experience, but by concentrating, he soon got the hang of such matters as long division, fractions, and decimals. By the end of the school day, he was even able to work his problems while the younger children were chanting their letters in shrill chorus.

At four o'clock the minister closed the session with another passage from the Bible. Later he joined Tom and Jed, who were pitching horseshoes out by the barn, and at their invitation he got into the game. Rolling up his shirtsleeves, he whipped a ringer over the pin at the very first cast.

"Whew!" Tom exclaimed. "Guess we've got to be sharp to beat the Reverend at this, Jed!"

As the game progressed, it was soon apparent that Groom was an expert. He laughed about it, saying it must be a leftover from his misspent youth, before the call came to him to study for the ministry. Afterward he took Jed aside for a talk.

"I'm impressed by your diligence," he said. "You have a keen mind, yet I gather you have never spent much time at school, and from your speech I take it you're a New Englander."

Jed tried to explain the circumstances of his boyhood and his present situation as an indentured servant. "I want to learn, though," he added. "If I could read the Bible like you, I'd be mighty proud."

"I'll lend you some books," said the preacher. "All you need is more practice at reading. Also your penmanship will improve before the classes are over. What would you like to do in life, Jedediah?"

"Be captain of a ship," Jed answered promptly. "The sea's in my blood, I reckon, same as most Nantucketers."

The minister nodded. "How do you feel about this war for American Independence?" he asked. "You said you are a Quaker and go to Friends Meeting."

"I guess," said Jed, after taking a minute to think it over, "I'm against killing, even if it's a Hessian or a dirty Refugee. But it seems to me about the only way to be free of old King George's taxes is to fight. I mean—we've got a right to have some say in our government, and he's taken that away from us."

"You put it pretty well." Groom smiled. "I can't fight myself, but I'm hoping at least to be a chaplain with Washington's army. And," he added, "when it's all over, I'd like to build a little church, right here in South Dennis. There are several good Baptist families here—Ludlams and Corsons and Hands—and they deserve a church of their own, instead of riding all the way down to Middle Town."

That night, as he lay on his bed of hay in the barn, Jed thought more deeply about that conversation. His conscience was bothering him a little. He was a Friend and wanted to remain one, and yet all his Quaker upbringing had taught him to respect justice and resist injustice. The Friends who settled Nantucket had been rebels against the unjust treatment they received farther north. War and killing were wrong, but how else could the colonists defend their principles? Was it still a sin for him to want to strike a blow for liberty?

No ready answers came to him, but after a while he fell asleep. When he woke at sunrise, he was no longer troubled. It was a fine day, he had a healthy appetite for breakfast, and he would be going to school. Other matters seemed distant and unimportant.

That day the older pupils were given a serious talk on the history of their new country. The Reverend Groom was well read. He told them of Columbus and the early explorers, then described the settlements at Jamestown and at Plymouth. He talked about the troubles other colonies had had with the Indians and gave credit to the Quakers for the peaceful relations Pennsylvania and New Jersey settlers had enjoyed with the red men, up to the time of the French wars.

Finally he came to the British Navigation Acts and the harsh stamp tax that welded the colonies together in revolt.

"We are many different kinds of people," he said. "The Puritans of Massachusetts, the Cavaliers of Virginia— owners of great plantations and poor, hard-working farmers and craftsmen. Yet something in the air of this new land has bred a love of freedom in us all. I am hardly worthy to call myself a prophet, but I believe with all my heart that we shall win our liberty and found a new, united nation, destined to become one of the greatest in the world."

Even the little children were awed into silence by the intensity of his words. As for Jed, he felt his heart swell proudly. He knew he was living in stirring times. Later, when the minister asked the pupils to learn the Declaration of Independence by heart, he found the noble words came easily to his tongue.

At the end of the week, Jed walked back to the Townsend farm on Saturday afternoon, helped Shadrach with
the chores, ate supper, and was called into the study by
Amos Townsend.

"Does thee feel this school is doing thee any good?"
asked the old Quaker.

"I think so, sir. The teacher is very able and seems to
take an interest in me. I've learned more arithmetic, and
next week we're to start on algebra."

"Hmm. Well, we miss thy help here, but I guess we can
stand it for three more weeks. Has thee been to the
Landing to see how the schooner is coming?"

"No, sir. But Samuel Corson says she'll be ready for
launching in another two weeks."

When he had said good night, he took his bath and
went to bed. After the sweet-smelling hay, his little garret
room seemed hot and stuffy, but he was soon asleep.

It was raining when he woke the next morning, and
both he and the squire put on oilskins for the ride to
Meeting. The weather had little effect on the attendance.
All the local Friends families were represented, though
some of the women and small children had stayed at
home. Among the men, it soon developed, indignation
against the Refugees was mounting. Haystacks had been
burned at two more farms along the Tuckahoe, and several cows had been slaughtered on Peck's Beach. This, Jed
knew, was a stretch of wild sea island above Corson's Inlet,
where some of the farmers let their cattle run. In a calm
sea it was all too easy for a ship's boat to land and capture
fresh meat.

"I'm a peaceful man," said one of the Quaker farmers,
"but if these outrages continue, I aim to keep a loaded
gun handy. Anybody that fires my hay is liable to get a
charge of buckshot."

There were few who disagreed with him, for though
most of the Refugees' acts of violence were directed

51

against the homes of soldiers and militiamen, the Friends sympathized with their neighbors. It was becoming more and more difficult, Jed realized, for anyone to remain neutral in such a conflict.

The rain stopped by midafternoon, and after an early supper, he set off for South Dennis through the dripping woods. By the time he had made a little over half the distance, the setting sun was in his face, half blinding him. So it was that he almost stumbled over the thing in the trail before he saw it. With a shock he realized it was the body of a man past middle age, shot through the head. Jed thought he knew most of the neighbors, but this was a stranger to him. The clothes were travel-stained and damp, and a three-cornered hat lay a few feet away, a big, ugly hole through its rim and crown. But the most important thing Jed noticed was that the dead man wore riding boots, clean, with no trace of mud on them. The fact that he had been on horseback when he was killed was further borne out by the jumble of tracks around the spot, made by shod hoofs.

With a shudder, Jed started running. Twenty minutes later, he reached the Corson house and told his story between pauses to catch his breath. Samuel Corson mounted a horse and set out at once, with Jed, Tom, and the preacher following on foot. As they neared the spot, they met Mr. Corson returning. He was leading his horse, and the body hung limply across the saddle.

"Who is it, Father?" Tom asked, but the older man merely shook his head and strode on, grim-lipped. Soberly the little procession moved past the Corson gate and on up the road to Dennis Landing. The Reverend Groom had to leave them there, for it was time for Sunday Evening Service. Jed entered the tavern and looked about for Major Hand, of the Minute Men. He was not there, but after a moment the boy recognized Lieutenant Swain among the men seated at a table.

"Could you come outside, sir?" he asked the young officer. "Mr. Corson wants to speak to you."

Swain grumbled a little at having to leave his supper but followed him to the door. As soon as he saw what lay across the saddle, he took charge with soldierly efficiency. The inn parlor was cleared, and the body placed on a table. A doctor was summoned. And while they waited for him to come, Jed told his story in full detail.

"Did you hear the shot?" the lieutenant asked him.

"No, sir. It must have happened when I was still quite a way off."

"And you've never set eyes on the man before?"

"I don't think so—no, sir."

"Looks like he was shot by somebody that wanted his horse or his money," Swain commented. "But there could be another reason, if we knew who he was. I'd better look through his clothes."

The pockets yielded nothing, and since it was unlikely a man would be traveling without cash, Swain was sure he must have been robbed of more than his horse. It seemed strange, however, that there wasn't a letter or a paper of any kind to identify the stranger.

"What about his boots?" Jed suggested hesitantly.

With some difficulty the lieutenant pulled them off the stiffening feet.

"Hah!" he said. "Here's something!"

There was a sort of pocket inside the lining of the right boot, and from it Swain drew a small, folded parchment.

" 'Know All Men by these Presents,' " he read. " 'Ye Bearer is hereby Certified to be Jeremiah Budd, Courier for ye Committee of Safety, State of New Jersey.' And it's signed by Governor Livingston, himself! Boy, you had a mighty smart idea about those boots!"

Six

MAJOR Joshua Hand lived not far away, and he arrived at the tavern about the same time as the doctor. The
latter gentleman needed only a glance to pronounce the
man on the table dead.

"Probably didn't live but a second or two after he was
shot," he added. "Looks like a solid ounce ball from fairly
close range."

Major Hand, meanwhile, was staring at the bloody face.
"Jerry Budd!" he said softly. "So they got him at last."

"That's right," Swain told him. "We found this in his
boot." And he handed over the parchment.

"No other papers, eh? Likely he was carrying an important message, but it may not have been stolen. He used to
keep most secrets in his head."

The major went on to tell them more about the courier.
He had been in dozens of tight places, once riding un-
scathed through a whole company of Hessian troops. The
Loyalists hated him, of course, but up to that day he had
seemed to lead a charmed life.

"Well," said Major Hand at length, "that's enough talk.
We've got to find out what message Budd was carrying,
and who killed him, if that's possible. Lieutenant, you've
got a good horse. Take this identification and ride to
Colonel Cox, in Batsto. He's on the Committee of Safety.
If you don't find him there at the ironworks, he's likely to
be in Mount Holly, and you'll have to keep riding. It
won't be an easy trip, for Batsto's a good sixty miles, and
you can't get there in much under two days. But we have
to know if Budd was bringing a warning of some kind."

"Ay, sir," said Swain promptly. "I'll try to reach Beesley's Point tonight an' ride the rest o' the way tomorrow."

As he hurried off, the major turned to the Corsons and Jed. "Now," he said, "let's try to look over the place where you found the body before it's too dark."

He rode ahead with Samuel Corson, and the boys followed them at the best pace they could make. It was well past sunset when they came panting along the trail and saw the two men squatted on their heels, examining the ground.

"The killer was afoot," Hand announced. "There are only the tracks of one horse—fresh shod. If we can find the blacksmith that shod him, we might get more information. Now, coming to the man who shot Budd, we've found some footprints back o' that holly bush. He was pretty well hid. Probably fired when the courier was right abreast of him—only about five yards away."

"Do you think he knew who Budd was?" Jed asked. "I wondered if perhaps he just wanted the horse and what money he could get."

"That's possible," the major agreed, frowning a little. "But if it was a Refugee, I'd wager he knew whom he was killing."

Jed went to the place of ambush behind the holly tree and searched the ground. It was almost too dark to see anything, but he made out the print of a man's shoe, left fairly plainly in the wet mold. To his surprise it was a small foot—a full inch shorter than his own. Somehow it was hard to picture such a little man shooting another in cold blood.

Hand and Corson were eager to start back now, for night had fallen. Much to the boys' relief, they were given a ride home, one of them behind each of the older men.

Mrs. Corson couldn't be too cross with them, knowing how important their errand had been, and she had kept the supper warm. After Jed lay down on his bed of hay, his brain was still puzzling over the murder, but he seemed to be getting nowhere. At last he gave up, rolled over, and decided to go to sleep. And just as he was dozing off, a sudden image of the killer flashed across his mind. He saw Al Jukes, the renegade Tory—mean, rat-faced, so small that he was almost a dwarf. Jed remembered him hurrying along through the Great Swamp behind Joe Crutcher. Of the two, he suspected Jukes was by far the more deadly. And he was of the right size to leave that footprint in the mud.

Wide awake now, Jed lay there, his pulse racing. At that moment he was of half a mind to get up and go find the Major, but sober reflection told him all he had was a suspicion. He decided to keep his thoughts to himself and await developments. He was sure Hand would never let the matter drop till the murderer was found and punished.

School resumed the next day, and Jed had other matters to occupy him. The events of the past evening seemed to have been a remarkably well-kept secret. There was no excited buzz of speculation among the other pupils, so he gathered Tom Corson must have been warned to keep silent. The little ones droned their multiplication tables, and Jed and the older students practiced writing with paper and quill pens. No special effort was made to teach them to spell, for at that time spelling was largely a matter of individual taste. Even lawyers and college graduates might spell the same word two or three different ways in the same letter.

There was a new boy in school that day—a big youngster of seventeen, named Zeke Mulloy. He and his father had recently come to Dennis to work on the ships, and he didn't belong to one of the old county families. Perhaps for that reason, Zeke had a chip on his shoulder. He was sullen to the teacher and scornful of the other pupils.

When classes let out that afternoon, Mulloy came over to Jed.

"You're a Quaker, ain't you?" he said. "Bound out to ol' man Townsend. Quakers don't believe in fightin', do they? That makes 'em no better'n dirty Tories!"

Jed bristled but held on to his temper. "There's a difference," he said evenly. "You can stand for peace and still be a patriot."

"Huh!" sneered Zeke. "If you're a patriot, why ain't you in the the militia or helpin' build ships, like me? I reckon I know what's wrong with you—you're skeert to fight. Let's find out!"

Before Jed could answer, the other boy clouted him across the face. At that, Jed's patience snapped. He swung his right fist against Mulloy's jaw with all the strength of his anger behind it. Zeke was fully as tall as Jed and many pounds heavier, but the blow staggered him, and he nearly

fell. Red with rage, he gathered himself for a fresh attack, but at that instant Peter Groom intervened.

"Stop it!" he ordered, in a voice that stung like a whiplash. "We'll have no fighting here. Shake hands, the two of you, and cool off."

His erect figure and blazing eyes had the authority of command. Zeke Mulloy slunk away, muttering something under his breath, and Jed bowed his head in shame.

"I know," he told the teacher. "I should have turned the other cheek, but it's terrible hard to do sometimes."

The young minister smiled. "Some things," he said, "are more than ordinary humans can stand. Only a saint or a coward would have taken that, and I know you're neither one."

The news of the fight must have been spread by some of the children. That night, when supper was eaten and the milking done, Jed was taking a stroll up the road. He had not gone far when suddenly, out of the dusk, a broad-shouldered figure appeared.

"Your name Starbuck?" asked a deep voice. "I'm Elam Gandy, from up at the Landin'. Used to be a bay pilot before the war. Now I fish an' dig clams mostly. They tell me you was once a whaler. Are you handy in a boat?"

Jed was somewhat confused by all this. "I'm not afraid of boats," he replied. "And I reckon I can row well enough."

He could see the man's face clearly now—a weathered face with crinkles around the eyes and a friendly grin.

"I hear you're on the side o' liberty," said Gandy. "Ready to fight for it, seems like. How'd you like to help out on a little night raid against the Loyalists? Wait now —don't say no till you've heard the rest. There's a nest o' Refugees hangin' out up the Cumberland side o' West Creek. We aim to take a whaleboat up there tonight, but we need a couple more lads to help handle the oars. You

58

wouldn't have to do any shootin'—just row. Ought to be home an' in bed before daybreak."

"I don't know," Jed answered, in doubt. "I'm a bound boy, just going to school here. The man that holds my indenture wouldn't want me mixing up in this, I'm pretty sure."

"How's he goin' to find out?" asked Gandy. "None of us'll talk, an' you'll be back in time for breakfast tomorrow mornin'."

Jed still hesitated. But the longer he thought about it, the more he yearned to have a part in this adventure. "What time do you aim to start?" he asked at last.

"Soon as it's full dark. Come along with me, an' we'll get the rest o' the boys together. We've got our boat hid down the creek a-ways."

In silence, they walked up the dusty road to Dennis Landing. When they reached the tavern, Gandy motioned to Jed to wait outside while he went in. He was gone less than twenty minutes. Then he reappeared alone and led Jed across to a spot of deep shadow above the creek bank.

"They'll be comin' out," he whispered. "All is, we don't want to make too much stir about it. You never can tell if somebody in there is a spy."

Sure enough, men began strolling out of the inn door, singly or in pairs, bidding each other good night. Jed counted a dozen such casual departures and saw them go sauntering off in almost as many directions. Minutes passed. Then he became aware of moving shadows below them, near the water. Gandy plucked at his sleeve, and they scrambled down the bank to join the rest of the group. Without a word, the men set off along the narrow path that led down the creek. Soon they passed the looming mass of the new schooner on her ways. Then, in single file, they moved on into the marsh.

Jed had never been down Dennis Creek, but he knew it

59

took a winding course to Delaware Bay, four or five miles to the west. The path ran straighter, cutting off bends and saving distance.

There were a few old cedars in the area, but most of the time they walked with open sky over their heads and tall reeds screening the sides of the trail. Nobody did any talking. Occasionally a night heron croaked, disturbed by their passing, but for the most part there was silence over the lonely marsh.

As they progressed, Jed's eyes became more used to the night. He could see Elam Gandy's hulking shoulders a stride or two ahead of him, and he noticed that the big ex-pilot now carried a gun in the crook of his arm. Where and when he had picked it up, the boy could not tell, but he thought it must have been hidden somewhere beside the path.

The company had been moving along at a good pace for more than half an hour when the men in the lead halted and held up their hands for the others to stop. Jed looked about him in wonder. On all sides the bulrushes grew tall, but right ahead he saw water. It was a deep, narrow cove, completely hidden from the main creek. And there, pulled up above the tide line, was a long gray-painted whaleboat.

"Everybody ready?" asked Elam Gandy in a low voice. There were nods and grunts of assent, and the men moved quickly to slide the boat into the water. Some of them, Jed saw, wore the leather hunting shirts of the Minute Men. Six or seven were armed with rifles or muskets, and he noticed more than one long-barreled pistol tucked in a belt. The warlike nature of the expedition came home to him for the first time, and he shivered a little as he waited his turn to climb into the boat.

There were three rowers' thwarts, with two men assigned to each. Jed was on the middle thwart, pulling the port oar, and beside him was a husky-looking youngster of about his own age. The cove, it turned out, was too narrow for the long oars, and they poled the craft through the entrance, with Elam Gandy steering at the stern. The other armed members of the crew were crouched in the bottom, forward and aft. Once they were out in the creek, the boat made better time, for an ebbing tide helped the oarsmen.

Another half hour passed, and Jed felt the heave of waves as they neared Delaware Bay. There was a bar off the mouth of the creek, but Gandy took them past it with expert skill. Then they were headed northwestward, bucking the choppy waters of the bay.

There was no moon. Off to starboard, Jed could barely make out the loom of the land. He knew they must be passing the mouth of East Creek, and West Creek would be only a mile or so farther on.

Nobody in the whaleboat spoke, and the oars made hardly a sound in the well-greased tholes. Abruptly Elam Gandy pushed on the steering sweep, and they bore in toward shore. At that moment one of the men in the bow gave a warning "Hist!" All heads turned to port, and there, outlined dimly against the lighter gray of the water, Jed saw the hull and lofty mast of a good-sized sloop. She lay at anchor, hardly more than fifty yards off their beam.

Silently the whaleboat held its course into the narrow gut that marked the outlet of West Creek. Only when they were well away from the sloop did Gandy speak, and then it was barely above a whisper.

"That's the *George,*" he told them. "We might catch some big fish tonight!"

Jed was itching with curiosity but didn't dare ask what the leader's words meant. All he could be sure of was that the men around him were tense and edgy.

"Keep rowing!" growled Gandy savagely. "Stroke together! We've still got a mile to go."

Sweat was running down Jed's back, but he concentrated on pulling strong and steady. The minutes went by.

At last Gandy held up a warning hand, and the rowers rested on their oars as he steered slowly toward the west bank. The bow scraped on shell and sand.

"All right, boys," the steersman whispered. "You all know what to do. The 'Fox an' Hounds' is just a couple o' hundred yards up yonder."

Seven

As he stepped forward over the thwarts, Gandy leaned down to whisper in Jed's ear. "No need for you to come," he said. "Stay here an' watch the boat if you'd rather."

In another moment the boy was alone there in the shadow of the bank. Instead of being grateful for the leader's advice, he felt some resentment. After coming this far with the expedition, he wanted to see it through. There must be a path from the water's edge that the men had taken, and though they were now out of sight and hearing, he believed he could follow them.

As he groped his way toward the bow, his hand encountered some object clamped in a cleat under the gunwale. It was a boathook, old and rusted but set on a stout hickory staff. Not much of a weapon, he thought, but better than having nothing to defend himself with. He wrenched it loose and jumped ashore. The whaleboat had been made fast to a cedar stump and wouldn't drift away.

Jed hurried up the path, hoping he might be in time for some of the action. Suddenly he saw a huddle of dark, still figures just ahead of him. The crew was crouching there, waiting for something. Beyond, Jed could see a clearing and the lighted windows of a small tavern. From a dozen yards away, there came a muffled thudding sound and a kind of groan.

"He got him!" breathed a man just in front. "Gandy's knocked the sentry out with a gun butt!"

The leader reappeared and signalled them to silence. "There's talk goin' on inside," Jed heard him whisper.

63

"We'll sneak up close an' surround the house. I want to hear what they're sayin'."

One by one they darted across the sandy clearing and took their stations close to the walls of the tavern. Jed was one of the last to arrive, but he could hear a mumble of voices coming through the thin siding. "Why not Dorchester?" one voice asked. ". . . get up there 'fore daylight . . . militia's gone off to the Cohansey . . . whole town'll go up like a torch!"

Jed's spine tingled at the ominous words, but at that instant his attention was called elsewhere. A wailing cry came from the edge of the clearing. "Help! Rebels!" The sentry must have regained consciousness.

Gandy sprang to the side of the steps, his musket poised. In a few seconds the door was flung open, and the plotters began tumbling out. The first one was clubbed down, the second shot by another of the young patriots, and the next two threw up their hands in token of surrender. Meanwhile, there were noises from the rear of the house.

Jed ran around the corner brandishing his boathook and was in time to see several figures leap from a back window. In the flickering light of the taproom candles, he caught a glimpse of one tall fellow in a green uniform, dashing for the woods. A Minute Man fired at him and missed. He was followed immediately by two more Tories, who scuttled off in the darkness. And finally a heavy man in an apron tried to squeeze through the window. Jed caught his belt with the boathook and jerked him to the ground, then hit him over the head with the thick wooden shaft.

In less than a minute, the whole fracas was over. The patriots had taken four prisoners, including the sentry and the innkeeper—Jed's own captive. Two Refugees were dead, and three had escaped.

They searched the house for any remaining skulkers,

64

took a couple of jugs of rum and a baked ham as booty, and marched the prisoners back to the boat. Everyone was elated over the success of the venture—everyone, that is, except Elam Gandy. To Jed's surprise, he was gruff and silent.

As the boat neared the mouth of West Creek, heads were craned for another look at the sloop that had been anchored offshore.

"Hey!" Jed heard one of the men in the bow exclaim. "Look! She's makin' sail!"

The rowers lost their stroke trying to turn for a better view, and Gandy snapped at them savagely. "O' course she's leavin'," he said. "That man in the green coat that got away was her skipper—Cap'n Lowndes, o' the Royal Greens!"

* * *

The row back to Dennis Creek was made without further incident, and by three o'clock in the morning they had beached their whaleboat in the cove. Jed was so tired that his eyelids drooped as he went stumbling down the road to the Corsons' house. Behind him, at the Landing, a celebration was in progress. Through his drowsiness he could hear the beating of a drum and raucous voices raised in song. The youths who had carried out the sortie were bound to have their fun, whether the local citizens slept or not.

He fell into the hay and knew no more until Tom Corson came to the barn after sunrise.

"What's the matter?" asked the younger boy. "You sick? I had to holler three times 'fore you opened your eyes!"

Jed yawned and blinked. "What time is it?" he asked. "I must have been mighty sleepy. Dreamed I heard a big commotion, like the one when we got the news we'd licked the British at Saratoga."

"It was no dream," Tom told him. "They were really hootin' an' hollerin' up at the bridge. Maybe General Washin'ton has beat the tar out o' Clinton. I don't know."

Perhaps, Jed decided, he could keep his midnight adventure a secret, after all. Tom had been the one who worried him most, and he seemed to be safe there. He milked, cleaned the barn, washed up, and went in to breakfast. Mrs. Corson looked harried and upset as she served the pancakes.

"They'll bring the war right here into Cape May County if they keep this up," she complained. "Fighting for liberty is all right, long as they do it somewhere else."

"What do you mean, Mom?" Tom asked, mystified.

66

"Who's fightin' around here? Or are you talkin' about Jeremy Budd?"

"No," she answered sharply. "And if you don't know, I expect you'll hear soon enough. Finish your breakfast now. School will be starting in ten minutes."

Jed had gone out to the yard for a breath of fresh air when Nancy Corson approached him. "You look a bit tuckered, Jed," she teased. "Didn't get much sleep, did you?"

"I feel fine," he told her. "That hay isn't very comfortable, but I make out well enough."

Nancy laughed at him. "All right," she said, "I won't give away your old secret. But I was watching from the window when you went off with that man Gandy last night. Anyway, I'm glad you didn't get shot."

He was somewhat chagrined, but he had a feeling he could trust the girl to keep quiet. Together they went in to school.

Jed managed to stay awake through the morning session. At noon he found Zeke Mulloy in the yard with the other boys, telling them all about the raid at the "Fox and Hounds."

"I got out o' bed fast when I heard 'em celebratin'," he explained. "So I heard it firsthand. They s'prised the Tories an' beat 'em without losin' a man! A lot o' Refugees was killed, an' four was took prisoners. Wish I'd been there—I bet there wouldn't have been a single one got away!"

It was all Jed could do to keep his mouth shut, but he finally joined the group of young admirers and listened to Mulloy's bragging. At least it appeared certain that nobody in the whaleboat party had mentioned his name.

When Samuel Corson came home from the shipyard that evening, he brought a fresh piece of news.

"Major Hand's found the blacksmith that shod the

67

horse Budd was riding," he told the two boys. "'Twas Jonas Hewitt, down in Goshen. Seems he recognized the courier from Hand's description, and he says the horse was a good one—a black with a white star in the forehead and one white stocking on the nigh hind leg. Budd was carrying saddlebags, too—maybe with messages in 'em."

Young Tom's eyes were popping. "Jiminy!" he whispered to Jed. "We better keep a watch out for that horse! S'pose we were the ones that helped catch the murderer!"

" 'Tisn't likely we'll be the ones to spot him," Jed replied. "I reckon the major's got all the Minute Men in the county looking for that horse right now."

He said no more, but in his own mind he had an idea that the black horse was tethered somewhere in the Great Cedar Swamp, waiting to be ridden on some midnight mischief by the mean-faced little Tory, Al Jukes.

The general excitement that had gripped the Dennis Creek settlement died down after a day or two, and the rest of the week went by without incident. Saturday came at last, and as soon as school was out, Jed set out for the Townsend farm. Old Trumpeter came trotting out to meet him when he was still a hundred yards from the house. Then he saw Shadrach at the well, drawing water to fill the cattle trough. And Aunt Hitty waved to him from the kitchen door. It was good to be home.

At supper Jed told Squire Townsend the story of finding Jeremy Budd's body. The old Quaker was shocked and troubled at the thought of such a brutal crime so close to his homestead. He had already heard about the raid at West Creek, and that caused him less concern. In fact, he seemed pleased that a nest of Refugees had been wiped out. Word of the affair had come to him earlier in the week, and Jed had an uneasy moment when the farmer brought the subject up. But suspicion of the boy's involvement was the last thing in Amos Townsend's mind.

At Meeting the next morning, little else was discussed.

Most of the Friends present were ready to praise the action of the Dennis men, for their neighbors' boats and farm buildings had suffered heavily at the hands of Tory partisans. As one Quaker put it, "Thee and I don't feel killing is right, but the more Refugees they put in jail, the better."

Toward evening, as Jed went out to the barn to do his milking, there was a light rain falling. Shadrach complained that the damp was in his bones. "I got a misery," he groaned. "You finish up, Marse Jed. Me—I got to git in by the fire."

With that he hobbled off to the springhouse with his pail of milk, and Jed was left alone. He was stripping the last cow when he heard a faint noise, different from the monotonous drip of rain off the eaves. He lifted his head from the cow's flank and listened. Perhaps, he thought, he had heard a rat gnawing at the grain bin.

It was at that second that something struck him on the back of the head, and he felt himself falling through a whirl of stars and blackness.

*　*　*

Jed never knew how long he lay unconscious, but it could hardly have been more than two or three minutes. The first thing he felt was a hammering ache in his head. Then he became aware that someone was hauling him along through wet grass. Rough hands gripped his arms above the elbows, and his feet half stumbled, half dragged over the ground. He was too weak to struggle or even to call out.

Soon he sensed woods closing about him. Brush and briars tangled around his boots, and drops of water fell on his neck. After an interminable while, the men dragging him made a halt.

"Come on," a bass voice growled. "Ye kin walk now. Git yer feet under ye!"

Jed made the effort. His legs felt numb, but somehow he stood erect, swaying drunkenly.

"That's better," said the same voice. "Now—step out!"

As he tottered forward, Jed tried to see who his captors might be. Apparently there were two of them. One walked ahead, and in the rainy twilight he looked like a gnome— small and deformed. The other man was at his elbow, urging him along. A glance out of the corner of his eye showed Jed a huge, hulking figure, a head taller than himself. The boy's heart sank still lower then. He knew who had taken him prisoner. It was that choice pair of renegades, Joe Crutcher and Al Jukes!

Jed's head still throbbed, but some of the strength was coming back to his legs as he was led deeper and deeper into the swamp. The two men must know their way well. Even in the darkness they pushed ahead at a pace that took all his breath.

Much as he wanted to find out where they were taking him, Jed couldn't seem to keep his mind on it. There were blank periods when all he could remember was the pain in his head and the effort of struggling on. And when he regained full consciousness, he found himself blindfolded. After what seemed an endless time, they reached their destination. Jed thought it must be some kind of shack, but there was no clearing around it, and it appeared to stand in the middle of a thicket.

Jukes led the way to the door, jerked the blindfold off Jed's eyes, and pulled aside a deerhide curtain.

"Git inside!" he snarled. "Hold him, Joe, whilst I make a light an' take a look at the young fool."

Jed heard him strike flint and steel. Then a candle flame lit the interior of the cabin. Among the shadows Jed made out a rough slab table, a clay fireplace, and two heaps of dirty blankets that must be the Refugees' beds. There was no floor, only hard-trodden earth.

From a peg on the wall, Al Jukes brought a length of

frayed rope, and ordering Jed to turn around, he proceeded to tie his wrists firmly behind his back.

"Lay down!" he ordered, giving the boy a push.

Jed fell to his knees, then toppled face down on the ground. At once he felt the rope pulled tight around his ankles. He was as helpless as a trussed calf.

The two men mumbled together in low voices. At length he heard Crutcher say, "Sure, he's safe here. Durn near dead, ain't he? Looks like you hit him harder'n there was any need."

"The rebel scum!" Jukes spat out. "This'll teach him to run with that pack o' mis'able farmers from the Landin'. We'll git even tonight fer what they done at the tavern!"

"Let's git on with it, then," growled the bigger man. "I'll go saddle the hosses. When we're back, it'll be time enough to see what ol' Townsend's willin' to pay fer him."

Jed's brain was functioning more clearly now. The last remark gave him an answer to the question he had been asking himself—why hadn't they killed him at once and gotten it over? Amos Townsend had the reputation of being a rich man, and the renegades were hoping to collect a ransom!

After a minute or two, Jukes came over and felt the cords that bound the prisoner. He gave Jed a parting kick in the ribs, blew out the candle, and departed, leaving the boy alone in the dark.

Eight

As soon as he was certain his captors had gone, Jed began trying to untie the rope at his wrists. He pulled and strained and did his best to get hold of an end with his fingers, but Jukes had done a thorough job. The bonds held firm, and the only result was to chafe his skin till it was raw and bloody.

At last he gave up. He lay there panting, wondering desperately what was to become of him. Perhaps, he thought, there might be a knife, or something sharp, on the floor of the shack. Painfully he rolled across to the hearth, cold now, and felt around for anything he might use to cut his bonds. But all he could discover was a crumb or two of stale cornbread and a patch of grease.

He groaned and worked his way to a sitting position, facing the door. As he looked that way, something moved the curtain of deerskin. He heard it rustle, then caught a snuffing sound. And in the next instant, a big body charged at him, knocking him backwards. It wasn't until he felt a wet tongue licking his face that he realized his visitor was Trumpeter, the fox hound!

"Trump!" he gasped. "Bless that nose o' yours—you found me! Now, if only I could make you understand!"

He pivoted around on his rump, holding his bleeding wrists under the dog's nose. Trump licked at the blood, hesitated, then finally seemed to get the idea. His strong teeth gripped the rope, and he worried at it, twisting his head from side to side.

"That's it, boy," Jed groaned. "It hurts, but keep trying!" The hound let go, snapped again, and got a firmer grip. The boy cried out in pain, but he felt the fibers starting to give and held his arms steady. Two or three more agonizing jerks and the old rope parted.

"Oh!" Jed sighed. "It feels so good to move my hands again!"

Gingerly he brought them around in front of him, flexed his numb fingers, and went to work on the knots that held his ankles. In another minute or two, he was free.

"Trump," he said solemnly, "I'll never speak another cross word to you as long as you live. Only now we've got to find our way out o' here."

He had no flint and steel in his pockets and could find none on the table. So there was no way to light the stub of candle that still stood there in the neck of a whisky bottle. In any case, he doubted if anything in the shack would be of help to him. He hobbled stiffly over to the door and peered out into the blackness of the cedar brush.

The rain had let up, but the sky was still completely overcast. There were no stars to guide him. His one hope, it seemed, was that Trumpeter could lead the way out of the swamp. Gently and in endearing terms he tried to tell the old hound what to do, but Trump merely jumped up and licked his face.

Jed felt his way back to the place where he had been lying and groped about till he found one of the ropes that had bound him. With fumbling fingers, he inserted an end under the dog's collar and tied some kind of a knot. One thing that had worried him was that if Trumpeter did start for home, he wouldn't be able to follow. With the leash in his hand, he could keep close to the dog.

Once more he led the way outside. "Now, boy," he said, "we've got to go home. Home—you know—go find the cows!"

That was a familiar order, and Trump sniffed the ground and started off at once. To Jed's surprise he rounded the corner of the cabin and trotted to another structure—a kind of pole-and-bark lean-to, as near as he could tell. A strong odor of horse came from the place, but it stood empty now. When Crutcher spoke of saddling the horses, he had meant what he said.

"Trump," said Jed, almost choking with exasperation, "you know better! The cows—go find 'em!"

The hound gave a whimper, then set out again. This time he headed straight into the woods, and Jed felt more confident. He did his best to keep up, but Trump was able to go under bushes that whipped him across the face and over logs that tripped him. What with the ache in his head and his sore wrists, he was almost ready to lie down and quit.

Somewhere he got the courage to keep trying. Time passed, and he still had no idea where they were, but when his feet began squelching in swamp muck, he was sure the dog was a long way from the direct route home.

Trumpeter pulled harder on the rope and let out an excited yelp. He was evidently following the trail of some animal like a fox or a coon. Exasperated, Jed hauled him to a stop.

"Look here, you stupid pup," he groaned. "Can't you see I'm hurt? You've got to get me home, Trump— *home!*"

It was no use. The hound's tongue lapped lovingly at his hand, but he showed no inclination to go anywhere. In desperation, Jed started out of the boggy muck, hauling the dog after him. When he reached dry ground, he went only a short distance before he saw a gleam of light through the trees. It was faint and flickering, but a light, nevertheless.

He staggered toward it like a drowning man trying to reach a spar. Somewhere near him he heard an owl hooting, and the sound sent cold chills down his spine. Was he walking into another Tory nest? Somewhere he

74

had heard that they signaled each other with the cries of night birds.

Then, as he stood shaking, he was aware of a tall black figure between him and the light.

"You, boy," croaked a high-pitched voice, "what you doin' yeah?"

He couldn't have answered if he had wanted to. Beside him the hound cowered, the hackles rising on his neck.

"You got no cause to be skeert," the voice came again. "Ah'm Mammy Shanks, an' Ah kin see you plain. Mah eyes is cat's eyes, an' Ah knows you's de shipwreck' boy, boun' out to ol' Squire Townsen'. You been hurt, ain't you? Jes' foller me."

Vaguely, Jed remembered hearing tales of Mammy Shanks. She was supposed to be a witch, but few people had ever seen her. Shadrach wouldn't even mention her name for fear she might "put a spell on him." But Jed was desperate. He moved after the tall, retreating shape, pulling the unwilling hound behind him.

Shortly the light grew clearer, and he saw it came from the open door of a tiny house. There was a blazing fire on the hearth, and a great iron pot bubbled on the crane. Inside, Mammy Shanks turned to face him, and for the first time he had a good look at her. She was a coal-black Negress, very tall and gaunt, dressed in an ancient black bombazine that didn't quite hide her bare feet. But it was her eyes that fascinated Jed. They were a strange, deep yellow, like a cat's.

"You done run foul o' dem two picaroons," she announced in her rasping voice. "Lemme see yo' haid."

With strong, gentle hands she explored the bruise. "'Tain't broke," she said.

Two long strides took her to a cupboard in the corner, and when she opened it, Jed saw a row of jars, filled with strange-looking herbs. Quickly the strange woman took pinches of several of these and mixed them in a small pot with hot water from the cauldron. Next, from a bunch of huge burdock leaves hanging on a rafter peg, she selected one and soaked it in the brew. Then her long black fingers laid the wet leaf over the back of Jed's head, binding it in place with a clean rag.

For the abrasions on his wrists, she used a strong-smelling salve that stung at first but soon took away the pain.

"Now, boy," she said, "you jes' set still a li'l spell. You go'n' feel better soon."

Trumpeter was cowering at Jed's side. Now he began to growl, low in his throat. And through the door came an enormous black cat, its yellow eyes narrowing and its tail fluffing at the sight of the dog.

"Satan," ordered the Negress sharply, "git over by the fire an' behave yo'self!"

Seated on a slab stool she had pulled up for him, Jed stared at the flames and drifted into a kind of rosy haze. All the ache had gone from his head, and his worry about the Refugees had left him, as well. All that was in his mind was a sense of being warm and safe.

Mammy Shanks moved quietly about the cabin without disturbing him. It must have been nearly an hour before he woke from his half trance and looked around him.

"I reckon I'm all right now," he said. "Thank you for all you've done, but I've got to be going back to Townsend's before they get too anxious."

"You hush an' stay still," his nurse commanded. "Dat no-count Shadrach's sho' to come back to de barn. When he do, an' fin' you gone, he figgers you done took off fo' de Corson place. Nobody go'n' worry over you."

Jed's jaw dropped. The woman's knowledge of all that had happened was uncanny, and he began to believe she did have supernatural powers. But if she was indeed a witch, she was a kind one, with a true gift for healing.

"What about the milk?" he asked. "I left a whole pail of it when they dragged me off."

"Oh," she replied, "Ah spec' dey jes' call you careless." And for the first time she showed her white teeth in a smile that made her look far less threatening.

"You git a bit mo' res'," she went on. "After while Ah'll set you on de right road fo' South Dennis. No need to fret about dem Refugees. Dey's skeert to come anywheres nigh my house."

*　*　*

It was at the first gray of dawn that Mammy Shanks woke him. She was holding a bowl of some sort of corn-meal porridge, and in her other hand was a pitcher of sorghum molasses.

"Cain't give you no fancy food," she said. "But dis'll stick to yo' ribs, so eat up, now, an' we'll git started."

To Jed's surprise the porridge tasted good. He cleaned out the bowl and stood up, his legs feeling stronger under him. The tall woman gave him a pan of water to wash in, then carefully removed the poultice from his head.

"How you feel now?" she asked, and he was able to answer quite truthfully that he felt as good as new.

She nodded. "We better be movin'," she told him. "When we git to de trail, Ah'll sen' yo' dawg on home."

The path she took was well hidden in the brush, but it wasn't hard to walk on. As he followed her, he got to thinking about the young Kechemeche who had helped him earlier.

"Mammy Shanks," he asked, "do you know the Indian, Wagamissi, who lives somewhere here in the swamp?"

"He's mah frien'," she answered simply, and Jed was satisfied.

The distance they traveled must have been at least two miles, and the sun was up when they neared the familiar trail to South Dennis. She stopped while the woods still screened them.

"You know de way now, boy," she said gruffly. "An' don' be skeert o' dem picaroons. Dey done head no'th las' night."

Jed tried to thank her, but before he could get the words out of his mouth, she had disappeared like a black shadow. He turned his back to the sunrise and marched ahead, thinking of the strange events of the past night. It was just as well he didn't need to tell anyone his story, for he was certain not a soul would believe him.

Oddly enough, though he could hardly have had more than three or four hours' sleep, he felt fresh and well rested. When he got to the Corson place, Tom was just coming sleepy-eyed from the house. He hailed Jed, and they went together to do the morning chores.

Mrs. Corson chided him a little because his appetite for breakfast wasn't quite as good as usual. He laughed and said he had had something to eat before he started, and the answer satisfied her. It was a bit more difficult when the sharp-eyed Nancy caught sight of the red scars on his wrists.

"Jed Starbuck!" she exclaimed. "Whatever have you been doing to yourself?"

"Oh," he answered casually, "I had to go up in the Great Cedar Swamp. You know what those brambles are like in there."

She said no more, but he fancied he saw a doubting look in her eyes.

Jed applied himself to his studies with more than the usual concentration all through the day. As soon as school was out, he made an excuse to get rid of Tom's company and hurried north, up the road to the Landing. He hoped to find Major Hand at the inn, and this time he wasn't disappointed. He went to the table where the officer sat working on some papers.

"Could I have a word with you, sir?" he asked. "It may be important."

Major Hand glanced around at the half dozen men in the bar and suggested they go outside. They walked a few paces till they were well away from possible eavesdroppers.

"It's about those Refugees—Al Jukes and Joe Crutcher," Jed began. "They came to Squire Townsend's farm last night while I was milking. They knocked me out with something—maybe a pistol butt—and took me up in the Great Swamp. I wasn't in any shape to know where it was, but they've got a cabin in there. Horses, too. I wouldn't wonder if Jeremy Budd's black horse was one of 'em. Anyhow, they tied my hands and feet and left me there while they rode off on some mischief or other."

"How'd you manage to get away?" asked the major, obviously much interested.

"Our old hound followed me there and chewed the rope off my wrists." Jed held out his arms, and Hand whistled at the sight of the deeply chafed skin.

"So you got loose," he said. "And you found your way out, in the dark?"

"No, sir. I got pretty much lost, and my head was hurting so bad that I didn't have any idea where I was. Then Mammy Shanks found me, and the medicine she made took away the pain in my head. I slept a while, and this morning she steered me out to the trail."

"Mammy Shanks, eh? I've heard about her. Most of the folk hereabouts are afraid of her and say she's a witch."

"Well," said Jed stoutly, "witch or not, she was a good friend to me. And I can tell you one thing—she doesn't like the Refugees any better than we do."

"Do you think she'd show us their hiding place?" asked Hand.

"I don't know, sir. It would be worth trying, though, if we could find her house."

"Hmm," the major mused. "If we don't catch 'em any other way, we'll see about it."

Nine

Jed was barely able to keep awake through supper that night, and when he fell into the hay a little after sundown, he was asleep almost instantly. The next morning the strain and weariness were gone, thanks to his youth and a strong constitution. All that remained was a touchy spot at the back of his head that felt sore if he bumped it. And as the day passed, even that discomfort left him.

At noon, Tom Corson took his father's lunch up to the shipyard and ran all the way home with the news.

"Hey!" he panted. "They're goin' to launch the *True Patriot!* Tide'll be high around four o'clock, an' they'll slide her in then!"

Jed was as excited as Tom was. They resolved to go and watch the great event the moment school was out.

At three-thirty, as they hurried up the road, horsemen and wagons were already raising dust clouds all the way to the Landing. It seemed as if half the township meant to be on hand for the launching. The tavern was doing a roaring business, but the two boys didn't stop there. They ran down the path along the bank and found themselves a point of vantage in a tree, close to the shipways. Around the schooner, thirty or forty men were gathered, some holding mauls, waiting to knock out the chocks when the word was given. Others were applying tallow to the smooth timbers that sloped down to the water.

The creek was still rising as the tide flowed in. After ten or fifteen minutes, the boys heard the beating of a drum, up by the inn. Then a fife began to tootle, and shortly they saw a little group of militiamen marching down the path. They carried the new thirteen-star flag that had been approved by General Washington, and though some were out of step, they were striding out bravely in time with the fife and drum.

The shipbuilders hailed them with laughter and a few cheers. The cheers grew louder when a huge young man appeared, carrying a barrel on his shoulder. In the thick of the crowd, he laid it down on a trestle, produced a bung starter from his pocket, and invited them all to step up with their mugs. Soon the foamy beer was flowing freely.

"Now," said Tom with a grin, "I reckon the launching can start. If the creek isn't deep enough, they've got enough beer there to float her!"

The tide seemed close to flood now. They saw Captain Daniel Hand coming down to the Landing in his brass-buttoned blue skipper's uniform, and beside him, to Jed's astonishment, was the brown-coated figure of Amos Townsend.

Neither of the men looked up into the tree. They went directly to Samuel Corson's side, checked their big silver watches, and stood waiting. At a shouted order from the foreman, the workers gulped down their beer and came back to their stations.

"Ready!" shouted Corson. "Let her go!"

The mauls came down against the blocks, and the men ran for safety. Slowly the heavy hull began to move down the ways with a squeal of wood sliding on wood. Then she picked up speed and hit the water. There was a tremendous splash that drove half the creek up on the farther bank, drenching the spectators there. The schooner careened far over till Jed could see her keel, then righted herself on the returning wave, and heeled back, exposing her deck to view. A ragged cheer went up from all who had managed to keep dry.

It took a few minutes for the turbulence in the creek to subside, but in the meantime, the schooner had been made fast to a dock with mooring lines. Even without her masts and rigging, Jed thought she was a pretty sight.

"Come on," said Tom. "She's in the water. Let's go down an' see what they do next." And he shinnied rapidly down the trunk.

Jed didn't follow him. The reason was that he saw Squire Townsend and Captain Hand strolling toward the tree. Apparently they were discussing something important and meant to do it in private, away from the crowd of sightseers. If Jed climbed down now, he was afraid his employer might scold him for idleness, so he stayed there, hidden by the leaves. He wasn't trying to eavesdrop, but it was impossible to avoid hearing what they said.

"How soon does thee expect her to be ready for sea?" the old Quaker was asking.

"Not over three weeks—two if we're lucky," Hand replied. "I'd like to take a few prizes before the autumn gales are on us."

"Good!" said Amos Townsend, rubbing his hands. "Now, Dan'l, thee understands I don't want any of my money used for guns or ammunition or other instruments of death. Thee pay for those. My half will take care of building the ship."

Captain Hand chuckled. "I understand, Squire," he said. "My conscience won't trouble me, so you can let yours rest easy. Of course, if there are any profits, you may find it hard to accept your share."

"No, no," the older man told him hastily. "Thee knows I'm doing this as an investment. If there are profits, I'll take them."

"Well," the captain told him, "we know there are prizes to be had, and we're making all the speed we can. The masts are here, ready to be stepped—fine, straight pine from Pennsylvania. I've sailmakers at work on the canvas, and the six-pounders should arrive any day now. Meanwhile, my mate is scouring the county from Cape Island to the Tuckahoe, trying to collect a crew. I've told him to sign on any youngster he can find who has ever trod a deck or sailed a boat—fishermen, oystermen, and farmers, just so they know a halyard from a hoe."

Jed's heart beat faster at these words. Perhaps, he dared to think, there might be a chance for him to sail with the *True Patriot!*

* * *

That same evening something happened that drove even the excitement of the launching from Jed's mind. As he was heading back to the barn after supper, he saw a rider on a jaded horse plodding up the road and recognized Lieutenant Swain. The young Minute Man knew him and reined in.

"Could I get my horse a drink?" he asked. "I've done a heap of riding. Be glad to sleep in a bed tonight."

Jed watered the horse. "Did you find Colonel Cox?" he asked.

"Finally, yes. But he wasn't at Batsto, and I had to go all the way to Burlington to catch up with him. Can't stop to talk now. I expect the major's wondering what's become of me. I got some news for him, though."

With that he kicked the weary horse into motion and rode on. Jed, who felt he had some right to know what had happened since it was he who discovered the murdered courier, was hardly satisfied to leave the matter there. Five minutes later he was following the rider up the dusty road.

It was nearly dark when he reached the Landing, but the windows of the inn had a cheery glow. He went boldly to the door and opened it to look in. Several of the local Minute Men were gathered around the table where Major Hand and his lieutenant sat. Swain was busy eating—wolfing down food like a man who had been on short rations for a long time.

"So that was their plan," said Hand thoughtfully. "Burning the schooner on the ways would have been quite a victory for the king. And once they'd killed Budd and stolen his dispatches, they must have thought the job would be easy. I wonder what stopped 'em?"

"Likely Cap'n Lowndes scouted the creek," one of the Minute Men put in. "Remember, the shipwrights were workin' nights that week, an' it prob'ly looked too busy 'round here. Then, the way I figure it, they went on up to West Creek."

The major nodded. "That's possible," he replied. "Catching them while they were at the Fox and Hounds was a piece of luck, and it likely saved a lot of trouble up at Dorchester. You boys did a fine job there. It's just too bad Lowndes got away. No telling where he may be now or what devilment he may be planning, so I'm going to put a strong guard on the schooner. What about you, Spicer? Can you locate Brown and Jenkins and a couple of others and stay aboard the *True Patriot* tonight?"

"Ay, sir!" The militia sergeant saluted smartly and went out to gather a guard. And Jed, satisfied that he had learned what he came for, set out for the Corsons'.

He had barely crossed the bridge when he caught the sound of footsteps behind him, and thinking of the Loyalist plots he had heard discussed at the tavern, he quickened his pace almost to a run.

"Hey—Starbuck!" a man called. "Slow down. I want to talk to you."

Jed stopped, for he thought he knew the voice. As the man came closer, he recognized the broad-shouldered figure of Elam Gandy.

"Last time I saw you"—the bay pilot chuckled as he spoke—"you wanted to do somethin' for your country. Still feel that way?"

"Ay," said Jed. "What did you have in mind?"

"I'll come straight to the point. Cap'n Hand's made me

85

his mate, an' we're tryin' to get a crew together for the schooner. You showed the other night you were handy in a boat. How'd you like to sign on? We're sailin' under a letter o' marque, an' that means any ships we capture are prizes. I can promise you a fiftieth share. If we're lucky, it might run into quite a bit o' money."

Jed's eyes were fairly popping. "I'd give anything to go," he said. "But I can't sign on unless Amos Townsend agrees. I'm his bound servant, you know."

Gandy nodded. "I've talked to the cap'n about that, an' I reckon he can convince the old squire. Besides—think of it this way. You can likely buy your freedom with the prize money you get!"

"That's true," Jed replied. "But Mr. Townsend might think he'd be better off keeping my indenture, so it's not the kind of argument to give him."

"All right," the burly seaman agreed, "we won't mention it. But I'm goin' to count on you for the crew, an' you'll hear from me."

He gave Jed a hearty clap on the shoulder that nearly knocked him off his feet. Then he swung around and strode off across the bridge, humming an old sea chantey.

With his head in a whirl, Jed went back to his bed in the barn. For a long time he was too excited to sleep, wondering if his dream could really be coming true. At last, knowing the decision would have to be Amos Townsend's, he offered a brief but honest prayer that the old farmer might see the light. Then, feeling he had done all he could, he rolled over and slept.

That week and the next would see the end of the school session. Jed had a real desire to get all the education possible, and he worked at his lessons conscientiously. It was surprising what progress he had made in this short time. Working with figures came easy to him, his handwriting was improving, and he really enjoyed reading such books as the Corsons had. Among them were Bunyan's *Pilgrim's Progress* and some plays by a man named William Shakespeare. Jed didn't understand all of the words, but in some passages he found a grand music that stirred his imagination. Some day, when he was his own man, he vowed he would buy a book of Shakespeare and read it all.

On Saturday afternoon he tramped the trail back to Townsend's, thinking all the way of what he might say to soften the old gentleman's heart. When he reached home, there was still an hour before milking time, and he went directly to knock on the door of the study.

Amos Townsend sat behind the table, his square spectacles perched low on his nose.

"Yes, Jedediah," he said, "I'm glad to see thee's back from thy school. I trust thee's doing well."

"Ay, sir. In health and learning both, I hope."

He drew a long breath and plunged on. "They're working hard to rig the schooner and get her ready," he said. "But they're having a lot of trouble finding a crew. I've been offered a chance to sign on and help sail the *True Patriot*. Since thee's a part owner, I—I hoped—" and he stammered to a stop.

The old Quaker frowned, cleared his throat, then looked at Jed with a suspicion of a twinkle in his eyes.

"I've had word of this from Captain Hand," he said. "If thee has wondered whether I can spare thee from the farm work, I think it can be arranged. As thee says, I have an interest in the—er—schooner, and it might be well for me to have a representative on board. One other thing has occurred to me, Jedediah. It is possible there may be considerable profits from this venture. Thy indenture still has over four years to run, and I value thy services at twenty pounds a year, or a hundred dollars in Continental hard money. Does thee consider that a fair amount?"

"Yes, sir," Jed replied in a shaking voice.

"Then," the farmer went on, "any prize money that comes thy way may be applied to shortening thy term of indenture. For example, if thee should get as much as a hundred dollars, thee would be free at the age of twenty. I hope for both our sakes it is far more than that."

To Jed's astonishment, the old gentleman rose and held out his hand. But once the handshake was over, his smile changed to the usual stern look.

"Well," he said gruffly, "no need to stand there like a ninny. Thee has chores to do." And he turned back to his papers.

* * *

Jed found it hard to keep his mind on his schoolwork that final week. Every day during the noon hour he dashed up to the Landing to see what progress had been made in fitting out the schooner. She had her masts now and her rudder. On the dock, under a strong guard, were the four six-pounder guns that would be her armament. Much of the rigging was already in place. Day by day she looked more like a fighting ship.

When Saturday came, the Reverend Groom invited several of his pupils' parents to see them show off their accomplishments. Jed had no family present to watch, but he performed creditably, exhibiting his penmanship, working a problem on his slate, and finally reading a chapter from the Bible. Considering the meager schooling in his life up to that time, he had probably made greater progress in a month than any of the other students.

There was, of course, no graduation ceremony. But when the rest had gone home, the young minister asked Jed to stay for a minute.

"Teaching is a poor trade," he said, "for those who want to make money. But there are other rewards. Once or twice in a lifetime a teacher finds a young mind so quick to learn that it's a joy to behold—like a stalk of corn shooting up in the sun. I wanted to tell you, Jed, that you have given me that enjoyment. When the war is over at last, I hope you can go on to college. This young nation needs minds like yours."

Ten

THAT Sunday Jed made his preparations. Aunt Hitty had mended some old shirts, and as a present to him she had knitted two pairs of wool stockings. He had owned a pair of sea boots when the whaler was wrecked. Now they were several sizes too small, and mice had gnawed the salt-crusted leather, but that fact didn't worry him. In warm weather he would rather go barefoot on deck.

He had attended Meeting with Amos Townsend in the morning. Now, after he made up a bundle of his belongings and prepared to leave, the old farmer came to the door with him.

"Remember, Jedediah," he said, "I'm proud to have thee on board the schooner. But try not to kill anybody if thee can help it. Thee's still a Friend at heart, I trust."

As he hiked westward on the trail to South Dennis, Jed began wondering where he would stay until the *True Patriot* sailed. After the weeks he had spent at the Corsons', he felt he could hardly impose on them any longer. Of course, he had no money to pay for lodging at the inn, but he decided to go there anyway and see if he could find Elam Gandy. Just as he crossed the bridge, he caught a glimpse of Captain Hand heading down toward the shipyard, so he hurried his pace.

"Cap'n Hand," he called, and the skipper turned and recognized him.

"That your sea bag?" asked the captain. "Looks as if you're ready to sign on."

"All ready, sir. I just wanted to ask you if I could sleep aboard. You see, sir, I've got no money."

"I'd be glad to have you on the ship nights," Hand replied. "But how do you plan to get your meals?"

Jed was a bit disconcerted. "I'll make out, sir," he said, "if it isn't too long before we sail. I brought some bread and cheese from home, and my pockets are full of early apples."

Captain Hand laughed and slapped his thigh. "That's a good 'un," he said. "But when you run out o' those, I'll see you get some real vittles. Go ahead on board and sleep outside or in the fo'c'sle, whichever you'd rather. There'll be a few militiamen about, but I'll explain to them who you are."

Jed found a long plank running from the dock to the schooner's side and was soon on her deck. There was a good deal of disorder there, for the riggers had left loose ends of rope, nails, chips, and even pulleys lying about. Jed hesitated to clean it up, knowing they would be back at work next morning. It was a fine, warm night, and he spread his blanket up in the bow, away from some of the clutter.

The stars came out overhead and wheeled slowly westward over the foremast crosstrees. Crickets chirped in the reeds on the bank. Pleasant as he found it there on deck, Jed had trouble going to sleep, for his mind was filled with prospects of the voyage.

It was nearing midnight when he heard men's voices singing discordantly and coming nearer on the path from above the bridge. A three-foot bulkhead screened the deck where Jed lay. He got to his knees for a better view of the bank, and the light of a half moon showed him three figures reeling toward the dock. They must be the guard, he thought, coming to keep watch over the schooner.

As they approached the gangplank, he saw they were carrying muskets. The first one took a step or two on the springy plank, waved his arms wildly as he lost his balance, and plunged into the creek with a yell of dismay. The others roared with drunken laughter. At length they quieted down and set about fishing their companion out. And just at that moment, Jed slapped at a mosquito on his neck.

"Hey!" yelled one of the militiamen. "Who's that on the ship? Show yerself or I'll fire!" And without any waiting, he let off a musket shot that rattled the rigging.

Jed was angry. "Who do you think you're shooting at?" he shouted. "I'm a member o' the crew—here by orders o' the captain!"

"We'll see 'bout that!" the soldier on the dock replied. "Git out here where we can look at ye an' keep yer hands up!"

Jed moved aft, his arms stretched high. But before he came abreast of the gangplank, there was a sound of running feet on the path. A big-shouldered fellow appeared and faced the militiamen.

"Who fired that shot?" he rumbled.

"Me," admitted one of them. "Seen a stranger aboard the ship, Mr. Gandy, an' he didn't answer when I challenged."

"All right," Gandy said, turning to the deck. "Who are you?"

"I'm Jed Starbuck. Cap'n Hand told me to sleep aboard. I never had a chance to answer any challenge. He fired as soon as he hailed me."

Elam Gandy thrust his jaw close to the soldier's. "You drunken louts," he said savagely, "where were you when this boy came aboard? Up in the tavern, I'll wager. And you're so tipsy now that you fall in the creek! Suppose he'd been a Tory—he could have blown her to kingdom come while you were off gettin' drunk! I'm goin' to report you to the major. Now snap to it! Let's see you act like soldiers!"

He left them there and crossed to the schooner's deck. In the dim light, Jed could see a grin on his face. "I see the old man agreed to let you do some privateerin'," he said. "I got most o' the men I need now. There'll be at least ten—more likely twelve—not countin' the skipper an' me. You plan to live aboard till we sail?"

"If it's all right," said Jed. "I don't have cash to pay for a bed at the inn."

"Mark my words," said Gandy soberly, "you'll have cash before many months pass. Privateerin's a good way to get it. All right, boy, get some sleep. Those idiots'll leave you alone now."

He swung away and recrossed the plank, completely ignoring the crestfallen militiamen. Jed went back to his blanket, and in two minutes he was sound asleep.

*　*　*

The crew of the *True Patriot* began arriving the next day. Most of them were youngsters of twenty or under—lads who had been around the water practically all their lives. Jed knew two or three of them. Besides these, there were two older men. Ananias Foster was a grizzled sea dog who had sailed in coasting schooners and in his earlier days had been a whaler. He came from the Goshen Creek area. Aboard the privateer he would serve as bosun. Jed, who knew his Bible, chuckled over Foster's first name, for never in his life had he heard anyone who could match him in the telling of improbable yarns.

The other veteran was a thin, taciturn character by the name of Ephraim Stites. Like Gandy, he had been a pilot in Delaware Bay and the Great Egg Harbor waters.

The mate got them all together on Thursday and laid down the law. "You think," he said, "that this is a free country an' everybody can do as he likes. That's part way true. But on board a ship—most especially a fightin' ship —there has to be discipline. When the cap'n or the mate or the bosun gives you an order, you don't argue. You jump to it—smart.

"Now, most of you know a bit about sailin'. Once we get a line on you, there'll be two watches picked—the starboard watch is the skipper's, an' the port watch is mine. You'll be on deck four hours an' have four off, except in a storm or a fight. Then all hands are on deck till it's over."

When these fundamentals were understood, he called them together on the schooner and made them learn the ropes. Jed, who had served in a square-rigger, found the simpler fore-and-aft rig relatively easy. He was able to give some help to his friend Jonas Hewitt, who hailed from Middle Town and was one of the few really green hands. By the day's end, he had made sure that Jonas knew a brace from a stay and understood the various purposes of the running rigging.

The previous evening Jed had finished the last crumbs of his bread and cheese and eaten the final apple. He was really hungry. But now a piece of luck came his way. Jonas had an uncle and aunt living only a stone's throw from Dennis Landing, and Jed was invited there for his meals. Two things made it easier to accept their hospitality. First, he knew that Jonas was sincerely grateful for the help he had given him. And second, Mrs. Hewitt seemed to take real pleasure in watching a hungry boy do justice to her cooking.

By Friday the ballast was in the hold, and the four cannon were in place on the privateer's deck, squatting on their carriages with the tackle all rigged. Now Gandy started instructing the crew in serving and training a gun. First he selected the four gun captains. He took the number one gun himself, and Foster, the bosun, had number two. The third cannon was put in charge of Stites. And the last captain picked was a tall, serious young fisherman from Cold Spring Inlet. His name was Martin Schellenger.

Shorthanded as they were, only two others could be allotted to each gun. One hauled the tackle and swabbed out the barrel, while the other loaded the powder and shot. The captain did the aiming and firing. Jed found himself appointed loader for the first gun.

They were pretty ragged at the beginning. Captain Hand stood by, keeping the time with his watch, and made some rather caustic remarks. "Fifty seconds," he announced. "That was your gun, Mr. Gandy. The slowest one was over a minute. D'you know what they call average time in a man-o'-war? Twenty seconds—that's what! Come on, now. Let's try it again."

The other member of Jed's gun crew was Jonas Hewitt, slow and clumsy at the start but strong and eager to learn. Gandy gave him some hints, and his timing on the tackle became faster with every try. Jed, meanwhile, quickly mastered the trick of handling the powder bags and ramming home the shot. Everybody was tired by the end of the day, but all four crews had brought their time down to the neighborhood of half a minute.

The next day several more men showed up to join the crew, and Captain Hand quickly signed them on. They were oystermen from the Maurice River, farther up the bay, and all were handy at trimming sail.

Meantime, the riggers had finished their work. The new canvas was bent on Sunday morning, and everyone became eager to take the schooner to sea. The powder and shot were already in the magazine, and the water casks had been filled.

"Well, boys," Elam Gandy told the ship's company, "flood tide's at five o'clock this afternoon. We'll take her down with the ebb, so if you've got any good-bys to say, you'd better get 'em over with."

There were still a couple of hours before sailing time, and Jed decided to go down and see his friends, the Corsons. They were home from church and had eaten dinner, but both Tom and Nancy still wore their Sunday clothes, for there would be another service that evening.

He found the two young people sitting on a bench under a tree, talking to Peter Groom. Jed felt a little ashamed of his ragged, work-worn breeches and his dusty bare feet, but the others soon put him at his ease.

"I hear you're to sail this afternoon," the minister said. "I'm glad for you, Jed. I know how much you want to serve the cause of liberty. You may not have heard about it, but I'm to be congratulated, too. My orders have come to join General Greene's army as a chaplain. So I'll soon be heading south, where most of the fighting seems to be now."

"But," Nancy put in, "he's coming back. When the war's over, Reverend Groom has promised to help us build a church right here in South Dennis. And maybe he'll teach us again!"

"That's fine," said Jed. "Hope I can be here to get some more schooling."

"You'll be here!" Tom told him confidently. "And you'll prob'ly be rich, too. If the *True Patriot* has a lucky cruise an' takes a lot o' prizes, you'll have plenty o' money. Wish I was big enough to go, too!"

Jed laughed. "I doubt if I'll be as rich as all that," he said. "I'm just glad to be a member of the crew. If there is any prize money, though, my share might help me shorten my indenture. And when it's all paid off, I'll be my own man. So I aim to keep alive till that time comes."

He said good-by to Mr. and Mrs. Corson, to Tom, and the young minister, but when he turned to shake hands with Nancy, he found she had suddenly disappeared. Jed had had very little experience with girls, and he decided he never would understand them. Perhaps he had said something that offended Nancy, but he couldn't imagine what it was.

Still puzzled, he started off up the road, and it was only when he looked back, a hundred yards from the house, that he saw her waving to him from her upstairs window. He waved back and set off once more, feeling better.

Eleven

THE departure of the *True Patriot* on her maiden cruise
was hardly the proud occasion Jed had looked forward to.
Quite a few people were at the wharf, it was true, and flags
were waving and the fife and drum corps played "Yankee
Doodle." But after the moorings were cast off, the schooner
swung crosswise of the creek, and her rudder caught in a
mudbank. A good deal of hard hauling and cursing on the
part of her crew was required to free the stern.

The sails couldn't be hoisted, of course, since there was
no room for tacking in the narrow channel. They warped
her down, with half a dozen men on either bank holding
ropes to keep her straight. So she drifted slowly down with
the current of the ebbing tide. Such breeze as there was
blew from the west, allowing millions of mosquitoes to
rise from the marsh and make life miserable for the men
on the bank. Jed, sweating away at one of the ropes, hoped
the arrival of dusk would end their task. But Captain
Hand kept them at it till it was no longer possible to see.

Finally, as the tide neared low-water mark, the schooner
ran aground once more, and this time she was allowed to
stay there in the mud. They were well past Sluice Creek
but still some miles from Delaware Bay.

A few of the sailors went to bunks in the forecastle. Jed
tried it, found the heat like an oven there, and came back
to lie on the deck. Around him the crew slapped at mosquitoes, snored, or talked.

"I allus said," grumbled one of the Maurice River men,
"Dennis Creek was no place to build anythin' bigger'n a
skiff. Up our way we got room to use our sails."

Some of the local men resented his remarks, but after their labor of that afternoon, there was little they could say in rebuttal.

"Well," one of them answered at last, "we'll be clear o' the land tomorrow, an' then you'll find out what a Dennis-built ship can do."

After a while they went to sleep, but their rest wasn't a long one. At dawn the incoming tide was high enough to float the vessel again. The creek had widened considerably at this point, and the mate took the wheel, steering skillfully around the bends, as the current carried them seaward.

During that morning of drifting, the crew was given a taste of routine duty. The cook got to work in the galley, and the bosun put most of the men to swabbing the deck. At noon they were in the mouth of the creek, looking out over the broad expanse of Delaware Bay. There the cap-

tain dropped anchor, and he and Gandy chose the men for the two watches.

When the selection was over, Jed found himself assigned to the port watch along with his friend, Jonas Hewitt.

All hands were then ordered to weigh anchor and make sail. The new white canvas crackled as it was hauled taut; the halyards were made fast; and under main and foresail and a single jib, the schooner heeled to a freshening breeze. She was, Jed thought, like a gull that had been caged and at last could spread her wings.

The wind was a little north of west—a fair weather wind—and after two short tacks to clear the land, the schooner was able to make a southward reach of it. She cruised along, a mile or two offshore, with her new rigging creaking comfortably and the waves slapping under her forefoot. Jed knew again the exhilarating feeling he had missed in the last five years. Westward, the bay stretched away to the horizon, too wide at that point to see the Delaware coast.

The starboard watch had the deck at the time, so the men of the port watch could do as they pleased. Most of them had brought fishing tackle in their gear, and they began trolling with handlines over the side. Fortunately for Jed, young Jonas had two lines and was glad to lend one to his companion.

The schooner was moving slowly enough so that a weighted line could be dragged along the bottom, and soon they were pulling flounders aboard. Once in a while, a sea robin was caught, and though it was worthless for eating, the strips cut from its sides made good bait for bottom fish. Within two hours, more than forty tasty flounders had been pulled in and cleaned. That evening the whole crew reveled in a meal of fresh fish.

In midafternoon they had passed the old lookout tower at Town Bank, once used by the whalers and now by the

Minute Men. There they kept watch for British frigates and convoys. The tower was too far away to make out the figures of men, but the schooner's crew was cheered by the sight of a Continental flag waving. At once the captain ordered their own colors run up. The Stars and Stripes were kept flying until they were rounding Cape May Point, then were lowered again. All privateer skippers liked to keep their identity a secret in case they met an enemy ship.

Jed's group had the first night watch, from eight to midnight, and Gandy sent him aloft to the lookout post in the fore crosstrees. The sea had been fairly calm when they rounded the cape. Now it was picking up from the northwest, so that the schooner sailed close-hauled, her starboard rail close to the wave tops.

In the dusk Jed watched the shore slip by—Five-Mile Beach, Hereford Inlet, and the dunes of Seven-Mile Beach. Then, off on the dark rim of the sea to the east, he sighted a speck that could only be a sail. As soon as he hailed the deck, Elam Gandy came swarming up the shrouds, a spyglass in his hand.

"Topsails of a big ship, headed south," he said, after a close examination. "Looks like a king's frigate on patrol, but I'd better let the cap'n decide."

He called down to the bosun and sent him to notify Hand in his cabin. A moment later the skipper joined them aloft, and just then the moon, nearly full, came over the horizon. By luck, the strange ship sailed right across the broad golden disk as Captain Hand was looking through his glass.

"Full-rigged," he reported, "and under topgallant sails. She could be a big merchantman, but I think you're right, Mr. Gandy. Looks to me like a ship o' the line, and the less we see of her, the better."

He descended the ratlines and told the man at the wheel to hold his course, then went back into the cabin.

Midway of the watch, Jed was relieved and returned to the deck. Some of the crew had gathered by the longboat, arguing among themselves.

"We should ha' gone after her," grumbled a youth from Cape Island. "Ain't no doubt in my mind she'd ha' made us all rich."

"More like she'd made us all dead," another replied. "Don't you figger Skipper Hand knows a man-o'-war when he sees one? What do you say, Starbuck? You were the one that spotted her."

"I'm ready to take the cap'n's word for it," said Jed. "I never saw a British ship o' the line, and I don't much want to, long as we've got only four little guns against her seventy-four big ones."

When eight bells sounded and the watch was changed at midnight, Jed went to his berth in the forecastle. The northerly wind had put a chill in the air, reminding him that, after all, it was well along in August and sleeping on deck might no longer be comfortable. The stuffiness under the foredeck bothered him only a moment. Then his healthy young body succumbed to sleep.

It was still dark when he was roused by loud bellowing. "Port watch on deck!" the bosun yelled. "Roll out, ye lubbers!"

The worst part of the early morning watch was that the cook didn't rise till daylight. There was nothing hot to eat or drink. And that morning, with the wind still freshening out of the north, the deck was a chilly place.

Jed soon had enough exercise to warm him, however. He was sent with two others to take a reef in the mainsail, and under the mate's supervision, they finally accomplished the job. At the same time, the foresail was reefed, and the schooner no longer heeled so far to leeward. She did pitch a good deal as she met the waves on her port bow, and some of the greenhorns in the crew found out what it was like to be seasick.

"I know how terrible you feel," Jed told Jonas Hewitt. "It used to hit me the same way, the first day out o' Nantucket. You might as well get rid o' what's bothering you —only don't try it to windward! Come on down here to the lee rail."

Those who still were hungry finally got fed at the change of the watch, and Jed and a few others made a fairly hearty meal. The wind was shifting more and more easterly; the sky after sunrise had turned a sullen gray. It looked as if they might be in for a spell of weather.

Jed had hardly had time to go below when he heard a hail overhead. The lookout, it seemed, had raised another sail. There was only a moment's respite before all hands were called on deck.

"Look," said Martin Schellenger, pointing northward, "there she is! A brig, I make her. What do you say, Starbuck?"

Jed peered through the spray and drifting fog. "I guess you're right," he replied. "Only a couple o' miles ahead. Wonder if we'll give her a chase."

That question was soon answered. "You, Starbuck—Smith—Schellenger—get aloft an' ready to set topsails!" shouted the mate. "The rest of ye, shake out those reefs!"

The wind was lighter now but still northerly. High up on the foremast, Jed and his companions eased out along the yard and loosed the square foretopsail, then trimmed it over till it matched the tight angle of the close-hauled lower sail. Others were performing the same operation on the main topsail. And a second jib was run up. Under practically full sail now, the schooner bounded forward as close to the wind as possible, with waves crashing under her bows and spray sweeping over the foredeck.

"Come aft here, Starbuck," Gandy ordered. "Give the helmsman a hand with the wheel."

Jed had never steered a vessel of this size before, and he was surprised at the force it took to hold the wheel steady.

"She's makin' too much leeway," panted the quarter-master, a man named Jenkins, as he gripped the spokes. "Shallow draft an' ain't got enough keel. We're pullin' up on the brig, though."

"We must be pretty far up the coast by now," said Jed. "What land do you reckon that is over to the westward?"

"Don't know for sure, but I'd guess we're close to Barnegat Inlet. Look! Ain't the brig comin' about?"

It was true. The sails of the vessel ahead were slatting in the breeze as she started to tack toward the dim shoreline.

"Bring her about!" roared Gandy. "All hands to trim sail!"

Jed helped Jenkins wrench the wheel over, and for an instant the privateer hung in irons, head to the wind. But her fore-and-aft rig gave her a big advantage in tacking, and she was soon only half a mile from the brig, now lumbering along on a parallel course, almost due north of her.

"Makin' for Barnegat!" said the steersman. "There's Tories 'round the inlet. But we'll ketch her 'fore she gets there."

On this tack the schooner seemed to be pointing better, and the distance between the two ships was lessening fast. The captain was on the quarterdeck, as he had been since sighting the other vessel. Now he raised his speaking trumpet.

"Ready your starboard guns, Mr. Gandy," he ordered. "Call all hands to battle stations!"

"Go ahead," Jenkins told Jed. "I can hold her all right now. Get your gun loaded."

The number one cannon was in the starboard battery, just forward of the foremast, and Jed found the gun crew there, waiting for him. The gun had been hauled back, and in his absence Gandy had already rammed home the powder and shot.

"Sorry, sir," Jed panted. The mate merely nodded.

104

"Run her out," he said, and Jed helped Jonas at the tackle.

The brig was in full view now, and close enough for them to see the crew hurrying to and fro on her deck. More than that, Jed could see a swivel gun mounted on her forecastle. It was being trained on the schooner—a fact that made a chill run up and down his spine.

Gandy, of course, had seen it, too, but he stood there calmly, a slow match in his hand, waiting for an order from the captain. At that moment the crossed flag of England was broken out from the brig's main truck, and Hand called for their own flag to be run up. As it fluttered at the top of the halyard, Jed saw a sudden cloud of white smoke from the brig's swivel gun. Then, after a second, came the loud report, and something whistled through the shrouds, falling in a spout of water just beyond the schooner.

"Fire as you bear!" shouted Hand. "Number one first!"

Gandy sighted along the cannon, waited for the roll of the ship, and laid his match to the priming. Instinctively Jed covered his ears as the crashing report came. Then he stood peering through the acrid smoke toward the enemy ship. Slowly her fore topmast seemed to crumple at the crosstrees and fall to the deck in a tangle of canvas and rigging. The crew of the *True Patriot* let out a cheer, but Gandy merely growled an order to haul and swab the gun.

"Number two, fire!" came the captain's steady voice.

And even as Jed pulled the wet swab steaming from the barrel, the second gun let go. This time there was no visible sign of a hit, but the brig was falling off the wind, her bow pointing astern of them.

Swiftly Hand had the schooner brought about, and another shot from the swivel fell just short of the taffrail as she turned into the wind. Jed rammed in the powder bag and the round shot. By the time the port battery could be brought to bear, the number one starboard gun was ready once more, and its crew had time to take a breather and watch the fight.

"Look!" cried one of the port gunners. "Her wheel's smashed! That's why she can't steer."

"I reckon that second shot did some damage after all," said Gandy. "But her flag's still flyin'."

The two vessels were only a hundred yards apart now, in easy hailing distance, and Jed saw Captain Hand put the speaking trumpet to his lips.

"Surrender!" he shouted. "Surrender or I'll give you a broadside!"

There was no answer from the disabled brig. They could see men working frantically to rig a jury steering gear, and others, in her bows, were reloading the swivel gun.

"Port guns—fire both as you bear!" ordered Hand. "Take out her gun crew if you can."

The two reports roared out almost together, but a wave heaved the schooner, and both shots flew high, plowing through the wreckage of the fore topmast. Then the swivel fired again. The small cannonball took out part of the schooner's rail amidships and hurled splinters in all directions. Luckily no one was seriously hurt, though poor Jonas caught a sliver in the seat of his breeches that brought a yelp of pain.

The brig's yards hadn't been squared, and she yawed crazily at each puff of wind. Hand swung the schooner across her stern, so close that Jed could see the white, set face of the British captain.

"Brig, ahoy!" bellowed the Yankee skipper. "We don't want to kill you and your men, but at this range we can't miss. Haul down your colors!"

There were long seconds of uncertainty, and then the enemy captain gestured toward the flag halyards. One of the seamen hurried to lower the Union Jack.

"Mr. Gandy," ordered Hand, "take eight men in the longboat and board the brig. Send the prisoners back and keep enough of our boys to sail her. You'll be in command."

Jed was one of those picked by the mate. They lowered the longboat, rowed over to the other ship's side, and clambered to her deck. What they found there was a doleful sight. The brig must have been shorthanded, for only six seamen were left alive besides her two officers. The man at the wheel had been killed by the ball that shattered the steering gear.

There was no fight left in any of them. Meekly the prisoners got into the boat and were rowed to the *True Patriot*. Meanwhile, Gandy had kept five men aboard, and he set them to work making the brig seaworthy. Jed and Jonas went aloft to clear the tangle of rigging around the top of the foremast. The others found a length of cable and completed a workable steering arrangement with what was left of the wheel. Within half an hour the mate signaled Hand that he was ready to proceed.

They trimmed the sails to run southwestward on a quartering breeze. Gandy took over the helm, and they soon found that though they weren't as fast as the schooner, they could at least keep her in sight.

It was past noon now, but the prize crew were too elated over their victory to be hungry. At last Gandy sent one of the older men to see what he could find in the galley and dispatched Jed to search the cabin.

"Might as well know where the brig hails from an' what sort o' cargo she's carryin'," he remarked. "I'd go myself, but this contraption needs a careful hand."

Jed felt a thrill of excitement as he trespassed on the part of the ship usually sacred to her officers. Somewhat timidly, he opened the cabin door and tiptoed in. It was a small but neatly furnished compartment, with a real bed, a combination chest and desk, and a teakwood table.

The drawers of the desk were locked, but he pried the top one open with the big blade of his jackknife. There were a number of papers there, some of them evidently personal. But within a minute or two, he found what he was looking for—the ship's manifest. It was an official-looking document bearing a big seal and the signature of an Admiralty clerk. And it stated that the brig *Mary Jordan* was clearing the port of Kingston, Jamaica, bound for New York, carrying "105 bbls. Jamaica Rum; 40 hogsheads first quality Molasses; 20 hundredweight best White Loaf Sugar; and 3 tuns Madeira Wine."

He picked it up with hands that shook. Such a cargo would be worth a fortune! Two minutes later he was reporting to the mate, where he stood at the helm.

"Read it to me," said Gandy. And when he heard what was in the brig's hold, he, too, whistled.

"Pretty valuable cargo," he said. "If we can get it to a port where it can be sold, that is. Looks like the skipper aims to put in at Little Egg Inlet. That's about ten miles south o' here. You run up aloft an' keep an eye peeled, Jed. I'd hate to have some Britisher come along an' grab us 'fore we can get in."

Twelve

J ED perched in the main crosstrees and searched the horizon anxiously for signs of a hostile vessel. Far ahead he could see the spread sails of the schooner, pulling away before the wind. Her lead had now been lengthened to three miles, he judged. Astern and to the east he saw only the tossing gray of endless sea, for the sun had been obscured by clouds in the last hour.

He was beginning to breathe more freely when he caught a glint of white, up to windward. Watching it, he made sure it was a sail before he hailed the deck.

"How big is she?" Gandy called back. "An' how's she rigged?"

"Can't see her plain," Jed replied. "But I can tell you soon, for she's overhauling us."

The brig still had her main course and main topsail set, and the fore course was pulling reasonably well. But the loss of the fore topsail slowed her down. Gandy looked at the canvas and shook his head. With his skeleton crew, there was little he could do except hope they could reach harbor before they were captured. Jed knew what he must be thinking.

Meanwhile, the *True Patriot* continued to pull away. It seemed likely that she hadn't yet sighted the pursuing sail. Over to the west, the long line of dunes and beaches showed no gap that might mark an inlet. Then Jed looked astern again. The oncoming vessel was no longer hidden by the horizon. Her canvas towered high, and he could make out courses, topsails, and topgallant sails.

"Looks like a full-rigged ship!" he called down to the

mate. "And she's making double the knots we are. I'd say she'd be in long gun range in another quarter of an hour."

"All right," said Gandy. "Ain't much doubt she's British, but keep an eye on her an' see if you can spot her colors."

It was strange, Jed thought, that the lookout on the schooner hadn't yet sighted the pursuing ship. Then he realized that the brig herself was blocking the view. The three vessels were almost in a direct line.

Suddenly he saw the schooner, now three miles to the south, veer to starboard and head for the coast. He called this news down to the quarterdeck.

"She's makin' for the inlet," the mate answered. "It's goin' to be nip an' tuck if we get there before we're captured. That ship astern is a frigate, sure as a gun's iron!"

A glance at the following vessel showed Jed a glimpse of color, flashing at intervals between her upper sails, and from what he could see of it, he was certain it was a British flag. He shivered at the thought of what a frigate's big guns could do to the helpless brig.

Gandy shouted to the other crewmen to trim the yards. "We've got to make a broad reach of it," he told them. "You, Starbuck—come down here an' help me steer!"

Powerful as he was, the mate was sweating as he wrestled with the broken wheel. The cable they had bent to the rudder chains creaked and strained but held fast. And as the sails were hauled in at an angle, the two helmsmen succeeded in bringing the brig over on a long slant to starboard.

The wind began to freshen now, heeling her lee rail down. Astern of them, Jed saw the big square-rigger swing smartly over in a maneuver similar to their own, and she was now barely a mile away.

"There's another inlet this side o' Tucker's Island," Gandy panted. "Doubt if a British ship would know it, so I'm goin' to take a chance. Even if the tide's up, it'll be a tough passage. There's bars an' shoals most o' the way across, an' just one tricky channel. Well—here goes!"

He gave a mighty heave on the wheel and yelled to the crew to trim the yards closer. They were on a beam reach now, headed straight for a narrow opening in the dunes.

"*Boom!*" The sound of a cannon shot came down on the wind, and a huge fountain of water rose, not far from the brig's stern.

"Just about in range," the mate grunted. "All right, boy —there's the surf ahead. You better start prayin'."

They seemed to be moving straight into the turmoil of white water on the bar, and Jed held his breath. But at the last instant Gandy gave the wheel a wrench. The brig's bow veered a little, and she entered a gap between the breakers that looked hardly a hundred feet wide. The passage of the reef may have taken a dozen seconds. To Jed, it seemed like an hour. Twice the ship struck bottom with a jarring thump, but each time the next wave lifted her off the shoal, and she staggered on.

Then suddenly they were inside, moving through calmer water. Another cannon shot screamed over, tearing a hole in the main topsail, but compared with the dangers of the bar, this seemed like a small matter.

"Bring her into the wind!" roared Gandy. "Come, boy, give me all you've got!"

They put their full weight on the rickety wheel and forced the brig's head through the wind till she was on the port tack. Meanwhile, working desperately, the men had horsed the yards around.

"If the old girl can hold together," said the mate, "we'll be out o' range behind the dunes in a minute. Cap'n Hand wanted us to head for Chestnut Neck, but he didn't know we'd be chased. Our best chance now is Tuckertown."

They beat northeastward, close to the outer island, for half an hour, then brought the brig about for a five-mile reach across the bay. Fortunately, the tide was at flood, for there were some shallow spots before they got to the mouth of the creek leading up to Tuckertown.

"Look!" said Jed. "There are masts over yonder, and some kind of a dock. Here comes a boat out now."

An odd-looking skiff with a single sail came skimming down to meet them. In it were half a dozen men with guns.

"You Yankee or Tory?" the fellow at the tiller asked truculently.

"I might ask the same o' you," Gandy replied. "I reckon you heard that British frigate firin' at us. What do you think we are?"

"Just had to be sure," said the boatsteerer. "That brig don't look American built."

"That's right," Gandy told him. "She was captured by the privateer *True Patriot* this mornin' off Barnegat. We're the prize crew."

"Good enough!" the man in the boat answered. "I'm captain o' the port. You can anchor where you are, or you can sail on up to the dock if you don't draw more'n three fathom."

"Well"—Gandy chuckled—"I guess we can make it to the dock. We come in over the bar, so maybe we scraped a bit off our draft!"

The brig had been lying nearly motionless, with her head to the wind and her canvas flapping. Now the mate eased her off till the sails drew again and brought her slowly in alongside the wooden pier.

It was nearly sunset before all the canvas was furled. With food they found in the galley, the men made a scanty supper, and then Gandy left them to stand guard over the prize while he rode off on a borrowed horse. It was only half a dozen miles across country to the mouth of the Mullica, and he expected to find the schooner there.

To Jed's surprise, and somewhat to his consternation, the mate left him in command. "I don't know these folks," Gandy said. "Reckon most of 'em are on the right side, but there might be a few light-fingered fellows around. You better arm the boys an' stand watches."

"It's not the men here that worry me," Jed told him. "But where do you reckon that frigate is?"

Gandy grinned. "Well," he said, "I hope she's run aground tryin' to foller us. But more likely she's just cruisin' outside, waitin' for us to come out."

He mounted his horse and started off. Jed called the other four together and, with as much authority as he could muster, told them what their duties were.

"You've got your cutlasses," he said, "and there are two good muskets. Jonas and I'll stand the first watch. Then we'll wake you, and you're on guard till daybreak. Keep an eye out for anybody sneaking along the dock or in a boat."

The men brought blankets from the forecastle and lay down near the mainmast foot. Jonas went to stand in the bows, and Jed perched himself on the afterdeck, holding a loaded musket. The breeze had died down, but a damp fog was coming in from the sea, so he poured fresh powder in the priming pan, working by the dim light of the binnacle lamp.

One by one the lights in the cluster of houses on shore went out. The fog obscured the moon, and Jed sat in almost total darkness, shivering a little in the cold. Once or twice he started to drowse but jerked himself back to consciousness. It would still be several hours before he could change the watch.

He listened to the light slap of waves against the hull and the piling, alert to catch any other sound. Once he heard a faint noise that might have been made by an oar, but it wasn't repeated, and he decided it had been nothing but the creak of timbers in the wharf. He was just settling back to wait again when his ears caught the sound of a stealthy footfall behind him.

"Who's there?" he shouted, and sprang to his feet in time to see a shadowy figure moving by the taffrail.

"Speak quick," Jed ordered, "or I'll put a bullet through you!"

There was no answer. Jed lifted the gun and took aim at the trespasser, but before he could pull the trigger, the man vaulted over the rail and disappeared. There came a thumping sound as he dropped into his boat, then the rattle of oars. Jed ran to the stern and fired down into the darkness, more as a warning than in earnest.

After the echoing report, he heard a squeal of pain. But evidently the stranger was only slightly hurt, for he rowed off with rapid strokes into the fog.

The commotion had brought all four of the prize crew aft at a run. "What did you shoot at?" . . . "Who was it?" . . . "Did you hit 'em?" they clamored.

Shakily Jed answered as best he could. "Probably a sneak-thief," he concluded. "I heard him yell when I fired, so I guess I may have wounded him. Anyhow, I doubt if he'll come back."

Jonas was awed by what he considered his friend's bravery. "Dunno's I'd ha' wanted to tangle with him," he said. "What time is it, anyway? Aren't we about due to go off watch?"

Jed laughed. "I don't suppose it's more'n eleven o'clock," he replied. "You stay here with me if you want. I was pretty lonesome myself, if you want to know the truth."

They put in another hour of guard duty with no further sign of trouble. Then they called the others and went to get some sleep. The rest of the night passed peacefully.

At daybreak the self-styled captain of the port came down to the dock. "Thought I heard a gun go off in the night," he said. "Who was it done the shootin'?"

"I did," Jed told him. "Some man sneaked aboard from a small boat and wouldn't give an account of himself when I hailed him. He must have seen I had a gun, and he jumped back in the boat and rowed off. I fired just to let him know we meant business."

"Hmm," said the Tuckertown man. "Nobody from the village here, I'll warrant. Must ha' been a Refugee. I know—" He snapped his fingers. " 'Twas that devil, Joe Mulliner! Abe Cramer said he was hangin' 'round the tavern, over New Gretna way, last night an' likely heard about the brig."

The Cape May County men were impressed. Joe Mulliner's name was known all over South Jersey as one of the most dangerous Refugees alive.

"You're plumb lucky he didn't have a pistol," said the port captain. "He'd as soon murder a man as eat breakfast."

The mention of breakfast made the prize crew remember they hadn't eaten. Two of them got to work at the galley stove and produced a meal that was at least edible. One thing they had found in the locker was coffee—a luxury none of them had tasted since the war began, and they all enjoyed a mug of the steaming black brew.

An hour later they heard a horse trotting down the road to the wharf. Elam Gandy was back, and the villagers had already told him about what had happened in the night. As soon as he came aboard, he got the full facts from Jed.

"If 'twas Mulliner," he said, "you can lay to it he wanted just one thing—to burn the brig. One man can't steal a barrel o' rum or a hogshead o' molasses. Chances are he'd heard about our takin' a prize in that tavern where he was seen. Anyhow, I reckon you gave him a scare."

He went on to tell them the *True Patriot* had heard the gunfire from the frigate, and Captain Hand was sure the brig had been sunk or captured.

"He was right surprised when I turned up." The mate chuckled. "He's bringin' the schooner here by the inside passage, an' the auction'll be here at Tuckertown 'stead o' Chestnut Neck."

Since she had to wait for the tide, it took the *True Patriot* most of that day to reach the anchorage off the dock at Tuckertown. As soon as Captain Hand came aboard, he had the brig's hatches opened and went down to the hold himself to make sure her cargo was as represented.

When he came up, he was rubbing his hands in satisfaction. "It's all there, just as it's written in the manifest," he said, "and as near as I'm able to tell, it's in good condition. Lucky our fire didn't hull her. Mr. Gandy, you and your men did a fine job to bring her in safely."

Later, after consulting with the port official, he told the crew the sale would be held in three days. "There'll be a representative of the Continental Congress here," he said, "and I look for a few merchants to bid on the cargo. I think we can expect some pretty substantial shares."

Thirteen

THE captain and mate were fairly generous with shore leave while they lay there at anchor. Every man in the crew had at least one day to stretch his legs and eat such landsman's food as was served in the little tavern. A few of the older hands took the opportunity to get drunk as well, but most of the youngsters were satisfied with ham and eggs and milk or cider.

Meanwhile, the men who stayed aboard were kept hard at work. They repaired the schooner's rigging, holystoned the decks, and polished the brasswork. By the time the auction was held, the *True Patriot* was fit as ever and ready for more action.

Only the ship's officers attended the sale of the brig *Mary Jordan* and her cargo. Apparently the bidding was spirited, and the rich Philadelphia merchants were prepared to go high for such desirable merchandise. Jed heard later that the ship herself was sold for $6,000, a fair enough price considering her condition. But the rum and molasses, the sugar and Madeira brought far more. The grand total came to more than $20,000 in hard money. Of course the Congress got half of that amount, but a good $10,000 was left as the privateers' share.

Jed was grateful for his recent month of schooling. He had no trouble figuring his own share as at least $200. And that would be two full years off his term of servitude! He also let himself dream of further riches, for after making such a capture in the first week at sea, he could hardly be blamed for imagining it would always be that easy.

It was Gandy who put a damper on his enthusiasm. "No

118

tellin' what's ahead," the mate remarked. "That kind o' luck won't hold, you can wager. Might be months 'fore we see another sail, an' if she turns out to be an enemy cruiser, we could all end up in a prison hulk—or Davy Jones' locker."

The *True Patriot* made sail again on the twenty-fourth of August, moving cautiously through the inner passage behind Tucker's Island and taking a good look at Little Egg Inlet before venturing out. The breeze was light from the northeast, and the skies were overcast. Hand had both topsails set as they made a reach of it out of the inlet, then filled away southward.

Up in the main crosstrees, Jed watched the gray ocean for a sail. What he feared most was to see that fast-moving frigate bearing down on them, for he had a mental picture of her lurking somewhere off the coast like a cat at a mousehole. It appeared, however, that she had been called away on other business.

The schooner was fast before the wind, and by noon they had passed Corson's Inlet, heading down the coast toward Cape May. Jed was just figuring that they might be in Dennis Creek by nightfall when he spotted a dot of sail on the southeast horizon. He called the deck, and as usual it was the mate who brought his telescope up to investigate.

"She's a two-master," he said, after a long look. "Seems to be fore-an'-aft rigged, an' no topsails. Could be a snow or a small schooner. I'll find out if the cap'n wants to look her over."

A moment later Jed saw the two officers consulting on the afterdeck. Then the mate gave an order, and the sails were hauled closer, while the steersman brought her over to a more easterly heading. No call was issued for the gun crews, so Jed stayed where he was. The fact that they were moving away from the familiar shore, with its many inlets, bothered him a little. The farther they went to sea, the less chance there would be for escape if a British cruiser appeared. Then he laughed at his own timidity. A privateer had to take risks if she wanted prizes.

The courses of the two vessels were converging rapidly, and so far the stranger showed no indication of running away. As Gandy had guessed, she was a small coasting schooner, apparently unarmed. At a distance of half a mile, Captain Hand had the colors run up and almost immediately called the gun crews. Jed, however, was told to remain on lookout.

From his high perch, he saw the smaller schooner suddenly come about. She was smartly handled, and in half a minute she was running southwestward before the wind. At the same time, Jed saw something else—a tower of white canvas that had rounded Cape May and was now only about four miles away. Much of her hull was visible, and he was sure he could see rows of black gun-ports in her side.

"Sail ho!" he yelled. "A frigate—broad off the starboard bow!"

At first his cry went unheeded, for both the captain and mate were shouting orders to ease off the sheets and bring the *True Patriot* before the wind. Jed waited till the uproar ceased and hailed the deck again.

"How far is she?" asked Gandy.

"Less'n four miles—about off Cold Spring Inlet—but she's coming fast! I can see her British colors now!"

The captain scowled and hesitated. Obviously he hated to give up what looked like an easy prize. But when Gandy pointed to the lofty sails now visible from the deck, he snapped out orders to bring the schooner around on the starboard tack.

Meanwhile, the smaller vessel they had been chasing was flying southwest, straight toward the big newcomer. It took no great wisdom to see that she had been used as a decoy, and Jed reflected bitterly that the scheme had almost worked. In fact, it might still be a close thing, for he knew the privateer was at her slowest when beating into the wind.

There was one chance for escape, and he could see Captain Hand was going to take it. Hereford Inlet lay some two miles due west. The schooner was heeled over on a beam reach, heading straight for the inlet. She would have to cross the frigate's bows within long gun range.

The mate called to him to come down, and he descended the ratlines like a monkey.

"May need you at the gun," said Gandy tersely.

Jed shivered, for he knew if it came to a cannon duel, their case was hopeless. In sheer weight of metal, the frigate outgunned them twenty times over. For the moment his orders were to stand by and help trim sail, and this he did with desperate earnestness. Falling off even a point or two might cost them all their lives. The *True Patriot* was making fair speed with a beam wind, and it seemed to him the strength of the breeze was increasing. The dunes of Seven-Mile Beach loomed higher now. They were less than a mile away.

How far off was the frigate? The question was answered a moment later when they heard the dull boom of a cannon. The shot fell nearly a cable's length short, but the fact that it was on line proved the skill of the Royal Navy's gunners.

"They must have a long twelve mounted for'ard," grunted the mate. "Time they can reload her, they'll be in range."

Jed held his breath, waiting for the next report. It came sooner than he expected, and this time the shot dropped near enough to drench the port side with spray.

"Hang on, boys!" shouted the skipper. "We're close to the inlet now!"

There were breakers off the port bow, but a lane of calmer water opened up dead ahead. The speed of their approach seemed terribly slow to the anxious crew. At last, as another shot screamed over, ripping the foretopsail, they lunged over the bar and on into the mouth of a narrow bay. And a dune on the southern side hid the frigate from view.

Jed felt weak and limp now that the strain was over. He knew the bigger ship could never make it across the bar, and for the present, at least, they would be safe from attack.

* * *

Captain Hand came to anchor some two or three miles north of the inlet. Good-sized trees on the island screened the schooner from view, and all they had to do now was wait.

Gandy called Jed to him. "You've shown you're a pretty good lookout," he said. "The skipper wants you to take one other man an' go ashore in the dinghy. You'll cross the island, pick out a good tall tree, an' climb it to keep watch. Whatever the frigate does, we want to know. Understand?"

"Ay, sir," Jed replied. "I'd like to take Jonas with me, if that's all right."

The mate agreed and saw that they were supplied with hardtack, oilskins, and a blanket apiece. "You won't need guns," he said. "All you're likely to find on the island is a few wild cattle."

Jed and his companion rowed across a hundred yards of water and beached the little boat in the reeds above the tide line. It was now well along in the afternoon, and from the gray skies a light drizzle was beginning to fall.

"We've got to find three things," Jed told Jonas. "A dry place to sleep, a good lookout tree, and a spring of fresh water if there is one. Let's get started."

As it turned out, they found water first. Two or three hundred paces from the spot where they landed, they came to a little pool with cow tracks around it. The water must have been fed by a spring, for it tasted sweet and cold. Each of them had a drink before going on.

The whole width of the island was only about half a mile, but in the middle it was high enough for a strip of forest to grow. There were oaks, gums, and hollies, along with the ever-present cedars. Jed picked out a big oak tree, not too far from the outer beach, and set about climbing it. Lying in the brush was a dead cedar with many gnarled bare branches. Jonas helped him lift it into place against the oak trunk, and from its top he was able to reach the lower limbs of the larger tree. After that, the climb was easy enough. He was soon in a crotch, fifty feet above the ground, with a good view of the ocean.

Misty as it was, and with dark coming on, Jed still had no trouble in seeing the frigate. She lay hove to, perhaps a mile offshore, hardly moving except for the slow roll of the swell. The distance was too great for him to make out the figures of men, but they must have been busy on the upper yards, for he could see most of her sails being clewed up. All she wore were her riding sails—a single jib and the mizzen topsail.

He watched for nearly an hour, till his legs were cramped and it was too dark to see more than the dim outline of the ship. At last he clambered stiffly down and looked about for Jonas. The other boy appeared after a moment, proud of his own accomplishments.

"I got us a good place to sleep," he said. "It's right up yonder in a cedar thicket. No rain comin' through an' nice dry sand to lie on."

They took their blankets and oilskins to the spot. Jed agreed it was the best place they were likely to find, and they were soon lying snug under the thick cedar boughs. Grateful as he was for being dry and warm, Jed began to feel a certain uneasiness. He sat up and nibbled a piece of dry hardtack.

"Maybe we ought to keep watch all night," he said, "even if it's too dark to see much. First, though, I'd better row back to the schooner and tell 'em what the frigate's doing."

He rose and stumbled back through the wet woods to the edge of the bay. Once in the dinghy, he had to guess where the schooner lay, for by now it was pitch dark. After a few strokes, he rested on his oars and listened. The tide was running out, and his boat was drifting south. Then he caught a faint sound of voices and knew they must be coming from the *True Patriot*. Steering now by ear, he pulled alongside the vessel and cautiously hailed the deck.

It was Gandy who answered with a gruff, "Who's there?"

"Jed Starbuck," he said. "I figured you'd want to know the British ship's hove to off the beach. Looks like she means to stay a spell. It's too dark to see her now, but we'll be back on watch at daybreak."

"Good enough," grunted the mate. "Go an' get some sleep now, if you can."

Jed made his way back to the island. Finding their camping place was more difficult, and at the last he had to call Jonas's name to get the direction. Then he crawled into his blanket and slept with a clear conscience.

It must have cleared in the night, for the sun rose brightly out of the sea and pierced the thicket to shine in Jed's eyes. He nudged his companion and started up.

"I've got to take a look at the frigate," he told Jonas. "See if you can find a cow with a calf. Milk would taste good for breakfast."

This time he didn't waste time climbing the tree but ran directly to the dune behind the beach. It was covered with tufts of stiff grass, and he could peer between the blades without showing himself. The frigate was still there, and he could see that now she had dropped anchor. The cable was stretched north from her bows against the running seas. The early sun was just astern of the ship, and it glinted on her polished brasswork. Grudgingly he had to admit she made a beautiful picture.

Then, as he watched, a good-sized boat was lowered from her side. It crept away from the frigate, headed toward the beach, and he could see the flash of sun on wet oars. Jed was thoroughly alarmed now. He ran at top speed back to the shelter of the woods and yelled for Jonas as he went.

There was no answer. But from somewhere far up the island came a bellowing of cattle that made his heart sink. He blamed himself bitterly for having suggested a foolish errand, though all he had wanted was to make his friend feel useful. At the moment, however, his duty was clear. He had to warn the schooner as quickly as he could.

Racing on across the island, he jumped into the dinghy and pulled with all his strength, heading for the privateer.

"What's up?" Gandy called when he was a few yards away.

"A boat!" Jed panted. "They've sent a boat ashore!"

"Nothing to be scared of," the mate replied. "They already know we're in here, an' if they start firing, we'll just move somewhere else. I reckon all they're after is fresh meat. We can't stop 'em from slaughterin' a little beef."

"That's just the trouble!" Jed told him unhappily. "I sent Jonas Hewitt to find the herd and get us some milk!"

"Hmm," said Gandy with a frown. "We got to find him 'fore they do. Wait till I tell the cap'n, an' I'll go with ye."

Fourteen

THE mate took the oars himself, and his powerful arms sent the dinghy flying through the water.

"We've got the tide to help us," he said. "Make better time in the boat than on land."

Jed watched the shore flash past and knew the mate was right. In a matter of minutes, they were a mile up the shore and nearly opposite the entrance to Great Sound. The occasional lowing of cattle came to them clearly now. Gandy swung the bow toward the island and beached the little craft.

"Come fast an' quiet," he told Jed. "If the men from the frigate are up this far, we don't want to run foul of 'em."

Together they hurried inland through broken patches of woods. Then suddenly Gandy halted, holding up his hand. Right ahead of them Jed saw an open grassy glade where fifteen or twenty cattle were huddled in a circle, horns turned outward. It was obvious why they were in this position of defense, for young Jonas was moving toward them, crooning, "So-o, boss—good cow!" in soothing tones.

"No shoutin'," Gandy muttered in Jed's ear. Then he stepped out into the glade and began whistling in a low key. At first he sounded like a bobwhite, but when the lad paid no attention, he switched to "Yankee Doodle."

Two bars of that were all it took. Jonas stopped and turned uncertainly. When he saw who was there, he would have yelled a greeting, but the mate was making frantic gestures for silence. Slowly the young sailor came toward them, wonder in his face.

Gandy and Jed each grabbed an arm, and they hustled him back into the cover of the woods. He was too surprised to speak at first, and when he did start to say something, the mate whispered that he must keep his voice down.

"I had her all picked out," Jonas muttered. "One of our own cows—a brindle with a little calf. I was goin' to milk her if I could get her out o' the herd."

"I'm sorry, Jonas," Jed told him. "I shouldn't have sent you up here. Right now there's a boatload o' British tars ashore, probably looking for beef."

Even as he whispered the words, they heard distant voices raised in talk and laughter. The party from the frigate would soon find the cattle. Followed by the two boys, Gandy led the way south through the woods and headed for the dinghy.

"Doggone it!" said Jonas when they were safely out of earshot. "My paw's got six cows an' some calves here on the island. I knew 'em by the Hewitt earmarks—a cropped left ear an' ha'pennies under both ears. It makes me boil to think of 'em bein' killed by those durn lobsterbacks!"

"I know how you feel," the mate answered, "but maybe there's somethin' we can do about it. How many men d'you think were in that boat, Jed?"

"At least a dozen, I'd say—or maybe even fifteen."

Gandy's rapid pace soon brought them to the beached dinghy. "All right," he said, "I've got a plan. It may be dangerous, but I need your help. One of you stay here at the landin'. T'other one, cross over till you can see the beach, an' find out where their boat is. I'm goin' back to the schooner an' see if we can't work out a surprise. Be careful, now, but don't worry. We won't desert you."

They watched him row away, down-channel. "You don't mind if I do the scouting, do you?" Jed asked his comrade.

And Jonas, not a particularly venturesome lad, was quite willing to let him go.

A quarter of an hour later, Jed was peeping over the top of a dune at the long stretch of sandy beach. From that vantage point, he had a good view of the anchored frigate. Nearer, a few hundred yards to the north, he saw a long-boat pulled up on the sand. Only two seamen had been left to guard it, and they were lolling against the gunwale, looking anything but alert.

Jed took careful bearings on the location of the boat before he started back. As he recrossed the island, he could hear the cattle bellowing again, but the sound seemed to come from farther away. It was likely, he thought, that the herd had taken flight at the sailors' approach.

When he reached the bay shore, he saw Jonas standing close to the water, peering down the channel.

"Look!" Jonas told him breathlessly. "It's our own longboat comin'—an' she's loaded with men!"

Jed caught some of the other boy's excitement then. He could see half a dozen seamen besides the rowers, and they had muskets in their hands. They were coming armed and ready for trouble. Gandy was at the steering oar, and as he started to swing the bow in, Jed waved him back.

"They're farther up!" he called, trying not to shout too loud. "We'll run along the shore and show you."

The mate understood and nodded. Jed caught Jonas's arm and started him northward at a trot, trying to explain whenever he found enough breath.

"Got to get between the British and their boat," he panted. "Here—this ought to be far enough."

Once more he waved to Gandy, and the mate put in to shore, where the boys stood waiting.

"They only left two men with their boat," Jed told the mate. "It's on the beach, over yonder. All the rest of 'em are chasing cattle, up north o' here."

"Good," said Gandy tersely. "Come on, boys. Look to your primin' an' don't talk."

He led the party eastward till they were well into the woods, then turned north, striding along at a steady pace. They had gone perhaps half a mile and were near the glade where Jonas had found the herd when Gandy signaled them to halt.

"I think I hear 'em," he said. "Reckon they're busy skinnin' out their beef."

In the stillness Jed caught a subdued sound of voices. Then there was a louder laugh. "Oo wants the 'ide?" a man asked in a Cockney accent. "Wot we're arfter is the meat!"

"Spread out," Gandy whispered. "Don't shoot till I give the word. We want 'em for prisoners."

The Americans followed orders and began advancing in a line nearly as wide as the glade. At the edge of the woods, the mate paused to reconnoiter. A hundred feet away, the men from the frigate were gathered around, watching the butchers at work. Muskets lay here and there on the ground, and no guard had been set.

Gandy made a sweeping gesture with his arm, and the Yankee crew went in at a run. They were almost upon the enemy before they were seen.

"Drop your weapons!" the mate roared. "An' get your hands up!"

The consternation among the British tars was almost comical. The ensign in command of the landing party was a mere boy, no older than Jed. In a shrill voice he tried to rally his men, but they were unarmed and could do little but huddle and stare at the menacing Americans. When the ensign drew his pistol, a shot from Gandy's gun promptly knocked it out of his hand.

Within two minutes, the whole group of prisoners was rounded up and started marching south. While some of the privateersmen picked up chunks of beef, Jed and Jonas were given the job of collecting the weapons thrown down by their captives. Gandy turned over the command of the guarding party to Foster and, taking Stites with him, set off to catch the two sailors left on the beach.

* * *

There was an uproarious celebration when they all returned to the *True Patriot*. Fourteen men of His Majesty's Navy lay in irons in the schooner's hold, and there was enough fresh beef for a feast. Captain Daniel Hand was the only American who did no cheering, and Jed thought he knew why. It would be only a matter of hours till the frigate's officers became alarmed at the absence of the longboat's crew, and then there would be swift retaliation.

So he was hardly surprised when the captain ordered all hands to weigh anchor and make sail. The schooner sailed north, then west into Great Sound, and was soon a good two miles inland from the beach. There she came to anchor again and waited for what might happen.

By now it was about two o'clock in the afternoon. There came the muffled report of a gun aboard the frigate, and Gandy chuckled.

"Callin' the shore party home," he said. "They ain't real worried yet."

Another hour passed before there was more shooting. Then a whole broadside was fired, with the cannonballs falling like hail back in the channel. If the schooner had not been moved, she would surely have been blown out of the water. Jed watched with awe. The big ship's officers must have discovered what had happened by now, and it was certain they would never leave till they had taken vengeance.

The sky was still heavily overcast, and darkness would come early that night. About six o'clock, at the end of the first dog watch, the captain called Gandy to his cabin. When he came out, the mate got the crew together by the foremast foot.

"Boys," he said, "we're safe enough where we are for a bit. They can't reach us with their guns. But come morning, they may be sending boats to board us. Likely they've got men on the island watching us right now. This sound we're in is too shallow to take the schooner any farther, but Middle Town lies right over yonder, a mile or so by water an' another by land. Jonas, you know the town. I want you to row ashore in the dinghy an' fetch a company o' militia to the landin'. Have 'em there by ten o'clock, an' we'll turn the prisoners over to 'em. Can you do it?"

The boy hesitated, and Jed spoke up. "Is it all right if I go with him, sir? We can row faster that way."

The mate agreed, and they started at once in the gathering dark. On the west shore of Great Sound, there was a dock and a landing used by local fishermen. The two boys left the boat there and hurried along a path that led overland to the county seat. Jonas led the way to the tavern, and there they were lucky enough to find Colonel John Mackey with two of his junior officers.

Within a few minutes, the amazed colonel was told what had happened and given the details of Captain Hand's plan. At first he seemed doubtful that this pair of ragged youngsters were telling the truth. But Jonas was well known in the village, and a fisherman at the tavern verified the presence of the schooner in Great Sound.

"All right," Colonel Mackey agreed. "We'll round up enough men for a guard and be at the landing by ten, you can tell Captain Hand. We'll hang up a lantern to let him know we're there."

Jed and Jonas made the best time they could in the darkness and were back aboard the schooner by nine o'clock. There were no lights showing, and even the binnacle lamp was hooded. The tide, Jed noticed, was running strongly up the channel and into the sound.

After a few minutes of preparation, the longboat was put over the side and the prisoners brought on deck. Gandy looked carefully at the ropes that bound their hands behind them, then supervised their descent into the boat. Four armed guards embarked with them, and there were four rowers. The mate did the steering.

Jed, Jonas, and three other seamen had remained aboard with the captain. A minute or two after the longboat disappeared into the dark, they saw a glimmer of light on the far shore of the sound.

"That's the signal!" said Jed. "The colonel got his soldiers there on time!"

Captain Hand nodded. "It's good he did," was his reply. "We still have a tricky night's work ahead of us."

For a while Jed worried about what those words meant.

Then the boat returned, and he soon found out. All hands were mustered aft, and the captain spoke.

"We've got three choices," he said grimly. "One is to abandon the schooner, row ashore, and go back to our homes. I reckon none of us would like that. The second thing we can do is sit here and wait till we're attacked. That's sure to happen before long, and some of us will be killed. But there's one other way out, if we're bold enough to take it. We can drop down with the tide and sail out of Hereford Inlet before they know we're gone. There'll never be a blacker night than this, and now that it's started to rain again, I doubt if we can be seen from the island. We're lucky to have pilots aboard who know these waters well. They can lay us a course in the dark. But every man of you'll have to do his part, too. When I tell you to trim sail, snap to it as if your lives depended on it —which they will."

When he had gone back to his cabin, one or two of the sailors grumbled a little, thinking the plan was too risky. Gandy overheard them.

"Maybe," he growled, "you'd like to be put ashore. There's still time, if that's what you want. But you won't get much respect from your neighbors—and you'll lose your share in the cruise. Which'll it be?"

It took them only a moment to decide they would stay with the ship, and from that time on there was no more complaining.

The tide reached full a few minutes after midnight, and as soon as the cable began to slack, they weighed anchor. As quietly as possible the mainsail and foresail were raised, and a jib set. Then, in the dark and rain, the schooner moved slowly down the channel. Gandy and Stites did the steering, feeling their way with sure hands past one shoal after another. Nobody spoke, and when any man moved, it was on tiptoe.

It must have been close to one o'clock in the morning when they reached the lower end of Seven-Mile Island. There Captain Hand had the vessel brought into the wind while the crew scrambled aloft to set topsails. Jed was among them. When he returned to the deck, his heart was beating fast at the thought of what might lie ahead, once they had cleared the inlet. Had their movements been seen from the island? If so, they might be greeted at any moment by a broadside from the frigate!

The wind was freshening now. The sheets were trimmed for a reach across the bar, and the schooner began her race to freedom. Jed held his breath as they surged past the tossing breakers. Gandy, grim and steady at the helm, took her through without so much as a scrape, and almost before Jed knew it, they were slacking sheets once more for a southward run before the wind.

The schooner leaped along like a live thing, with the following seas breaking over her transom and drenching the afterdeck with spray. There was nothing but the black night to be seen astern, and they heard no booming of cannon. The only sounds were the howl of wind in the rigging and the crash of the waves.

For perhaps ten minutes after their dash through the inlet, the crew kept silence. Then a spontaneous cheer went up from every seaman aboard, and the officers made no move to stop it. They had made their escape!

Fifteen

AFTER rounding Cape May in the early morning hours, the *True Patriot* beat her way northward, entering the mouth of Dennis Creek just before dawn. For the next few days, she lay at anchor, a mile or two up the estuary, and during that time Captain Hand saw to it that the crew was kept busy. Each man was given one day of shore leave. Jed and Jonas, when their turn came, went directly to the Hewitt house at Dennis Landing and stuffed themselves with the good food Jonas's aunt cooked for them.

Word of their capture of the brig had traveled fast through the county. Now the main topic of conversation was the privateer's narrow escape from Great Sound, for her predicament had been told far and wide by the Middle Town militiamen. In the churches that Sunday, prayers of thanksgiving for the crew's safe deliverance were fervently offered by their relatives. And the two boys found that they were heroes wherever they went in the village.

Meanwhile, the schooner was being made ready for sea again. Water, provisions, and more powder and shot were carried down the creek in small boats and stored aboard her.

The county maintained an efficient system of lookouts, stationed along the bay shore and the seacoast, and they reported that the frigate had left her position off Seven-Mile Beach. As soon as daylight disclosed that the privateer was gone, the British scouts had been called in, the anchor weighed, and sails set. Briefly the big fighting ship had cruised into Delaware Bay. Then, finding no sign of her Yankee enemy, she rounded the cape once more and set a northeasterly course. Probably she was back on her patrol of New York Bay by now. At least that was the hope of all the *True Patriot's* crew.

Jed had no opportunity to visit the Townsend farm, but on the last day before sailing, Amos Townsend came to Dennis Landing. He was anxious about his investment, but he was also genuinely glad to see Jed.

"I've had some qualms of conscience," he said, "about letting thee go into so much danger, Jedediah. Has thee been well? Does thee get enough to eat?"

Jed reassured him on both points and made little of the perils he had been through. "Captain Hand and Elam Gandy are both fine seamen," he told his employer. "Any time we're in a tight place, we know they'll get us out. So don't worry about me—and be sure to give my regards to Shadrach and Aunt Hitty."

They sailed out on a Friday in the first week of September. The weather was sunny and mild, and there was a light westerly breeze to help them as they tacked across the bay toward Delaware, rounded Cape Henlopen, and continued southward along the coast. No sails were sighted that day. But the second morning, somewhere off the Virginia capes, a fast-looking schooner appeared to the south of them. Captain Hand ordered the *True Patriot* brought into the wind and swung to a northward course that would parallel the stranger's. She was still two miles away, and there was no way to tell her nationality or whether she was armed.

Both vessels were on a beam reach, and both seemed to be making about the same speed. By a little after noon, they were off the long, sandy island of Chincoteague. There were no other ships in sight.

"All right," Hand called out. "Let her fall off a bit. We'll cut across the schooner's bows and speak her."

As their courses converged, Jed, who was at the mast-head, could see some scurrying about on the other ship's deck. Soon a section of rail on her port side was dropped. At once he hailed the mate.

"They're loading a cannon, sir!" he reported. "Looks like a twelve-pounder."

Orders were given immediately to ready the *True Patriot*'s starboard battery, and Jed was called down to do his job. The two schooners were now only a quarter of a mile apart, still moving fast under full sail. Captain Hand had the American flag run up, then gave the other ship a hail through his speaking trumpet.

"Schooner ahoy!" he shouted. "Show your colors and heave to!"

The British jack was already being hoisted on the other vessel. Now an angry reply came back. "Sheer off, there, or I'll fire!"

"Hold your course," Hand ordered the steersman. "Starboard guns ready!"

The bigger gun aboard the British schooner was fired first, and the solid shot plowed clear through the *True Patriot*'s forecastle. Luckily all hands were on deck, and nobody was killed.

"Fire as you bear, number one!" the captain roared. Gandy sighted quickly and put the match to the priming. At that range he could hardly miss, but he had purposely aimed high. The six-pounder shattered the other ship's main mast near the truck, hurling splinters among her men and cutting the halyards, so that the gaff fell all the way to the deck. With the mainsail blanketing her after-deck and burying half her crew, the schooner seemed to be in a serious plight.

The *True Patriot* was right alongside now. "Strike your flag!" cried Hand. "Surrender in the name of the Continental Congress!"

137

Actually the colors had fallen along with the mainsail, but the British skipper came of a hardy breed. "Never!" he shouted. "You'll have to sink us first!"

Captain Hand had no such intention. Any ship willing to put up a fight must be a good prize. He ordered grappling hooks thrown, and when they were fast and the sides of the two vessels were grinding together, a boarding party under Gandy was ready to leap the rail.

Only half a dozen enemy seamen met the attack, firing their muskets wildly. One Yankee sailor, a youth named Godfrey, fell wounded, but the rest quickly overpowered the Britishers and disarmed them before they could re- load. The captain, red-faced with rage, fired his pistol, waved his sword, and jumped over the rail.

"He'll change his mind," said Gandy calmly. "Throw him a line, Foster."

The bosun heaved a rope toward the floundering cap- tain, and, sure enough, he grabbed for it. They hauled him in like a fish.

While the prisoners were being secured and the main- sail furled, Jed and Jonas carried young Godfrey to a mat- tress on the deck of the *True Patriot*. There was no sur- geon aboard, but Ephraim Stites had some skill with wounds. He took the musketball out of the lad's shoulder, washed the hole with clean sea water, and put on a band- age.

"That'll hold ye till we make port," he told the white- faced youngster.

Their prize was the *Kestrel*, out of Barbados, carrying a cargo of rum for the British in New York. Her main top- mast would have to be replaced, but she was still able to make four or five knots. This time Jed was not in the mate's prize crew. He was kept aboard his own vessel to nurse the wounded Godfrey.

With the wind still favoring them, the two schooners cruised northeastward past the Delaware capes, and some thirty hours after the capture, they entered Great Egg Inlet. Once safely inside, Captain Hand sent the prize upriver to May's Landing, where she and her cargo would be auctioned. The *True Patriot*, meanwhile, tied up at Beesley's Point. There Godfrey was visited by a local doctor, who cleaned the wound, applied fresh dressings, and pronounced the patient in reasonably good shape.

The privateer's forecastle was a shambles. However, the crew, aided by two ship's carpenters from the Tuckahoe River, tore out the smashed timbers, rebuilt the broken bunks, and soon had the damaged section usable again. Jed found there were some advantages in being in port. The cook was able to get fresh milk and eggs—even an occasional loaf of bread baked in a Dutch oven in some farmhouse kitchen ashore. So the fare was much more appetizing than the hardtack and salt beef they usually got at sea.

It took nearly a week to assemble the buyers at May's Landing. On the appointed day, Captain Hand sailed the *True Patriot* up the winding course of the Great Egg, arriving in time for the sale. Once more the bidding was brisk. The *Kestrel* and her cargo of rum brought a combined total of $12,600, and Jed happily figured that with his share he would be able to cut another year off his indenture.

The representatives of the Continental Congress gave special praise to Captain Hand for the prisoners he had taken aboard the schooner and on Seven-Mile Beach. At that time the British held too many Americans in the filthy prison hulks at New York, and they could only be released through an exchange of captives.

It was on Monday morning, ten days after they had left Dennis Creek, that the schooner returned to Great Egg Bay and set her course for the open Atlantic once more. The wounded Godfrey had been left with a family on shore, who would take him down to his home by wagon once he was well enough to travel. Otherwise, the crew were healthy and eager for more action.

A sea was making up outside. This seemed surprising to Jed, for the puffs of wind on the surface were still westerly. High overhead, however, he could see clouds racing up from the southeast, and the air had a heavy feel to it.

Gandy, of course, had noticed the same signs. "Might be workin' up to a storm," Jed heard him tell the bosun. "But the skipper'd like to try our luck up the coast again, an' there's always inlets where we can put in for shelter."

They ran north past the beaches of Absecon and Brigantine and sighted nothing that looked like a sail. A little after noon, Hand ordered the schooner brought about. The wind had shifted now, and the clouds were thickening, and he preferred to be in familiar waters if the weather grew worse. As usual, Jed was acting as lookout in the fore crosstrees.

A few miles south of Great Egg Inlet he made out a sail ahead and hailed the deck. Then, even as Gandy was climbing with his spyglass, they heard the dull boom of a distant cannon. The mate came hurrying up the ratlines and pointed the glass toward the southwest.

"It's a big sloop," he said. "Seems to be firing at somethin' smaller that I can't see yet. Wait—there it is, on top of a wave—a whaleboat full o' men! An' there's another, just beyond!"

Close-hauled, the *True Patriot* bore down on the battle, her guns loaded and run out. At a distance of a mile, they could see British colors flying from the sloop's tall mast. She let go another cannon blast, and one of the two whaleboats was hit amidships, throwing her crew into the angry sea.

Several men were still struggling in the water when the schooner drove down on them, headed sharply into the wind, and tossed lines to the swimmers. The maneuver took precious minutes, but Jed was glad when four survivors were pulled aboard. They gasped out their story as they lay dripping on the deck.

"It's Cap'n Lowndes an' his Tories," one man said. "They come ashore an' burned some houses, so we put out after 'em."

"Man your guns!" ordered Hand. "I'd rather catch Lowndes than the richest prize on the coast!"

Standing ready at the forward gun, Jed stared at the sloop, now only a cable's length away. He recognized the name on her transom—the *George.* It was the same sloop he had seen off West Creek the night of the raid on the Tory tavern.

Both vessels were rolling and pitching in the rising seas, so that accurate aiming might be difficult. Captain Hand ordered the starboard guns to fire as they bore. But before the mate could use his slow match, there came a deafening blast from the sloop's nine-pounder, and the deck leaped under their feet. Jed regained his balance and ran to the rail. The shot had smashed a gaping hole in the schooner's side, just above the waterline. He hurried back and told Gandy what he had seen, but the mate was busy sighting his cannon. He fired on the rise, and the ball flew high, tearing through the enemy's mainsail. The number two gun was more effective. Its shot hit the carriage of the *George*'s cannon and slewed it around, out of commission.

Now the two ships were only yards apart. "Grapple her!" yelled Hand. "Soon as we're fast, board her!"

The grappling hooks were thrown and hauled tight, and the starboard side of the *True Patriot* hit the *George*'s port side with a crash. Thrown to the deck, Jed jumped up again and seized a boarding pike—the only weapon at hand.

He was the third or fourth man to make the leap to the sloop's deck, and a sudden pitch of the vessel threw him heavily on his back. As he started to rise, a cutlass blade

142

hit the side of his head. That was the last Jed saw of the battle.

* * *

He struggled back to consciousness, after what might have been minutes or hours, and found himself lying in a narrow space of deck, looking up at a mast and rigging that swayed across the sky. Someone was bathing his head with rum. The sickening fumes of it made him retch, and the sting of the alcohol gave his wound such pain that he cried out. Then the man who had been doctoring him departed, and he was left to puzzle out, with his tired brain, where he was.

There was no more firing, so he decided the fight must be over. But the vessel on which he lay had only a single mast. Had the *True Patriot* lost a mast, he wondered dully? No, he knew with a sinking heart that he must be aboard the enemy sloop!

The deck was pitching fearfully. He could hear shouted orders above the howl of the wind and tried to figure what they meant. It sounded as if the Tory crew were trying to beat to windward, but the gale and the big seas made it difficult. At that moment, a huge wave came over the side and washed him into the lee scuppers, where he nearly drowned before he could catch a breath.

Now the shouted commands sounded more and more frantic. It must be that the sloop was being driven on a lee shore—but where? With the wind from the northeast, it could only be Peck's Beach, a lonely sandy stretch below Great Egg Inlet. Jed had never heard or felt such wind. Its force was so great that seamen on the deck were blown off their feet unless they found something to hold on to.

Slowly he worked his way up to a sitting position, clinging to the rail. His head still hurt, but he was no longer faint or dizzy. One look to leeward and he knew the sloop was doomed. Through the scream of wind came a more ominous sound—the thundering roar of breakers, now only a hundred yards away. The crew must have tried to put into Corson's Inlet and failed.

Then, a few feet away, a man appeared, coming forward from the sloop's cabin. He was tall, grim-faced, and held himself erect in spite of the crazy motion of the vessel. And the green uniform coat told Jed this was the notorious Captain Lowndes. He wore his sword, and under one arm he held an oilskin package—probably the ship's papers. He moved along the heaving deck, speaking to the men in a voice Jed could not hear because it was drowned out by the hurricane.

The mainsail ripped away in tatters with a sound like an explosion, and seconds afterward the sloop broached to, taking the full power of the seas on her beam. The deck canted at a forty-five degree angle. Then she struck, side on, with a sickening crash, and Jed felt himself catapulted into the surf.

Strangling, fighting for his life, he swam with all the strength left to him. Once or twice, as his head came above the water, he gulped a little air. Then a breaker would overwhelm him again and pound him into the hard sand below.

At last, more dead than alive, he was washed up on the beach amid a welter of wreckage from the sloop. Painfully he crawled a few yards higher, and once more weariness blacked out his senses.

Sixteen

THE lash of rain on his face brought life back to him. The gale was still raging, and the storm-driven tide was washing around his feet. It was nearly dark.

Huddled close to the dune, twenty yards farther north, he could see the bedraggled survivors of the *George*'s crew. Some lay exhausted; others thrashed their arms against the cold wind. The sloop was on her side in the surf, with wave after tremendous wave breaking clear over her.

Cautiously Jed moved his arms and legs. Nothing seemed to be broken, and though his head throbbed painfully, he thought the blood had stopped flowing from his wound. Through the wind-driven rain and the dusk, he looked again at the group of Tory sailors. None of them seemed to be paying any attention to him. Very likely they thought his body was merely another of the several corpses washed in by the sea.

On his belly he began inching his way up the slope of the dune. It was a slow process, with many pauses, and by the time he reached the top the night had become really dark. He could no longer see the sloop's crew and was sure they couldn't see him. He crept over the crest and lay panting in the shelter of a twisted old cedar.

If he had reasoned correctly, the *George* had gone ashore on the south side of Corson's Inlet. That would be the upper end of Ludlam's Beach—a long, desolate island, stretching seven or eight miles between Corson's and Townsend's Inlets. He knew little about it except that near its southern tip was the saltworks, owned by Amos

Townsend. If he had the strength, he might try to reach that familiar place. Certainly he couldn't stay where he was, for the Loyalist crew would be sure to search the area once the storm ended.

So Jed hauled himself to his feet and started south. On the lee side of the dune, there was a growth of bayberry and beach grass that hindered his progress, but at least he was partly protected from the force of the gale. He went slowly, feeling his way and stopping occasionally to rest. He was thirsty, and there was salt crusted on his lips, so he turned his mouth to the whipping rain and managed to catch a little moisture.

After an hour or more, the wind suddenly dropped. The high surf still beat like thunder on the shore, but the scream of the gale had died. Looking upward, Jed could see a star overhead. He was in the "eye" of the hurricane. He had heard of this phenomenon before and knew the calm would last only a short time. An hour or less, and then the wind would blow again from the opposite direction. He must make as much distance as he could before the raging gale returned.

So he pushed on. The walking was easier on the seaward side of the dune, where his bare feet encountered nothing worse than broken clam shells. Far behind him, up the beach, he saw a glimmer of light. The crew must have found enough driftwood and dry powder to start a fire after the wind and rain stopped. He tried to estimate the distance and thought he had come about two miles.

Exactly as he expected, the sky blackened again, the rain began to fall, and the wind came in mighty gusts from the landward side. If anything, he thought it blew harder than before. He crouched lower under the crest of the dune and stumbled on.

Jed lost all track of time then. All he knew was a stubborn determination to keep his weary legs moving. Twice he fell, exhausted, and lay for minutes trying to recover his strength. At last, as the night wore on, the hurricane blew itself out, but for a time he hardly noticed that the buffeting of the gale had ceased.

Now he had a new problem. In several places the tide, driven into the bays behind the island, had completely covered the ground. Channels had even been cut through the dunes, and sometimes he had to wade waist-deep across rushing torrents.

After an endless time it was daybreak, and he saw the shattered remains of a windmill a mile ahead. It could only be the saltworks, and the sight gave him new energy.

As he drew slowly nearer, he must have presented a strange sight to the saltmakers. His shirt and breeches were torn to rags, his hair was a loose mop over his eyes, and the wound above his temple was a mass of caked blood.

The men at the works were lolling about as usual, amid the wreckage of the salt plant.

"Great jumpin' crabs!" one of them exclaimed. "What sort o' critter's that, comin' yonder?"

Another man squinted at him closely. "By thunder," he said, "it's the bound lad from ol' man Townsend's. However'd ye git in such a fix, boy?"

Jed merely stared at him. "Where's Dr. Harris?" he muttered thickly.

The fellow chuckled. "Went ashore yestiddy," he replied. "Missed the big blow. He'll shore be in a tizzy when he sees what happened here!"

Jed eased himself down on the edge of one of the salt pans and stared about him. One of the buildings had been smashed to kindling wood, and the other was tilted off its foundation. The great pans themselves were full of rain water, and there could be no pumping done until the windmill was repaired.

"Have you folks got anything to eat?" he asked.

"Ain't likely. The cookstove was in that house that blowed apart. Why—you hungry?"

"I guess not," Jed answered. "Just tired."

An hour later Dr. Harris came bustling up from the landing. He looked around him at the devastation, then told the men to get to work.

"It'll take a week to get back in operation," he said, "so this is no time to stand idle."

He turned toward Jed. "You aren't one of the workmen," he remarked. "Who are you?"

"I work for Mr. Townsend. Is there a boat I can use to get home?"

At least Amos Townsend's name had some effect. The manager hemmed and hawed a little, then told him he might use the older of the two skiffs at the landing.

Jed found it half full of water but succeeded in bailing it out. So tired he could hardly lift the oars, he rowed up the channel and across the flooded breadth of Townsend's Sound. When at last he beached the boat, he lay down on the reed-strewn shore to rest a little. There he fell asleep, and the sun was high in the sky when he woke again with a start.

Someone was standing over him—a tall, copper-skinned figure, naked above the deerskin breeches. It was his friend, the young Kechemeche.

"You hurt," said Wagamissi. "What you do here, white boy?"

Jed put a hand uncertainly to his wounded head. Rain had washed away some of the caked blood, but he knew it must still look serious.

"Just a blow from a sword," he replied. "Knocked me out and bled a lot, but I guess I'll live. I walked all the way down from Corson's Inlet in the storm. What brings you here, Wagamissi?"

"Hunt deer," said the young brave, and he held up his bow and quiver of arrows. "How long time ago you eat?"

"I don't remember. Some time yesterday, I reckon."

The Indian opened a leather pouch at his waist. "Here," he said. "Heap good meat."

What he held out to Jed looked like blackened sole leather, but when he gnawed at it, it tasted wonderful. He thought it must be venison, dried and smoked. Ravenous as he was, he could eat only about half the piece. Then he got to his feet, feeling more like himself.

Wagamissi accompanied him part of the way to Townsend's farm. Then, in the thickest part of the woods, he stooped, looked carefully at a spot in the forest mold, and waved Jed on his way. The Indian had found a deer sign. Without a sound he vanished into the brush and departed on his hunt.

Jed reached the farm just before noonday. He saw old Shadrach limping in from the cornfield with a basket on his shoulder and heard Aunt Hitty rattling pans in the kitchen. At the moment he reached the back door, she came out to call her husband to dinner. Then she saw Jed.

"Lan' sakes!" she cried in terror. "Whatever happen' to you, Jeddy? Look lak' you mos' daid!"

Before he could answer, she led him inside and started to work on his head with gentle hands. When the deep scalp wound was washed and bandaged, she insisted on his eating some fried chicken. Shadrach had come in, meanwhile, and sat across from Jed at the table.

"We thought you was gone," he said, shaking his gray head. "Cap'n Hand put in Her'ford Inlet las' night ahead o' the storm. He done sen' word to Mist' Townsend this mornin' that you was missin'."

So the *True Patriot* was safe! Jed was so glad to hear the news that he cheered.

"Where's Mr. Townsend?" he asked. "In the study?"

"He done rode down to Middle Town," Shadrach answered. "Wanted to talk to de cap'n, mos' likely."

"Then I've got to go, too," said Jed. "It wouldn't do if they sailed without me."

"You too dog-tired!" Aunt Hitty put in. "Couldn' walk that fur to save yo'self. Shad—you hitch up de wagon an' take him down."

Shadrach was only too glad to get out of more work in the cornfield. Behind the old mare, Brownie, they were soon jolting south on the dirt road to the little courthouse town. Jed tried to explain to the old Negro how he had been hurt and why he had left the schooner. But naval battles were far removed from Shadrach's experience, and all he could do was repeat over and over that the hand of the Lord had been in it. Jed had a feeling he was right.

When they were a mile or so above the village, they could see two tall masts far out in Great Sound, beyond the cedars.

"There she is!" Jed exclaimed. "Right where we anchored before. I'll get out here and foot it to the landing. And you'd better head for home before Mr. Townsend finds out you've been driving around in the wagon."

"All right, Marse Jed, if you says so," Shadrach replied unhappily. "But please try an' keep out o' that fightin' an' do a lot o' prayin'!"

A few minutes later, Jed had gone down the path to the landing and stood at the edge of the sound. The captain's boat was there, but it appeared he and the rowers had gone on to the tavern in Middle Town. Jed sat down on a driftwood log to wait for their return.

Fighting off the clouds of mosquitoes was all that kept him from drowsing again. But after half an hour he heard voices coming down the path. He recognized Elam Gandy's bass rumble, and apparently the mate was talking to Captain Hand.

"The old man took it sort o' hard, didn't he? Ye might think the lad was his own son."

Before Hand could reply, the group came into view and could see the boy sitting there by the boat.

"Speak o' the devil!" Gandy said in a hushed voice. "Do you see what I see?"

"Jed!" yelled Jonas Hewitt. "Is that really you?" And he dashed forward to greet his friend.

In a moment they were all around him, pouring out questions about his head wound and how he had managed to escape.

"Belay, there!" said Captain Hand with authority. "What can you tell us, Starbuck, about the *George* and her crew?"

"I was knocked unconscious," Jed replied, "but when I came to, they were trying to make it into Corson's Inlet, sir. The wind took her past, and she ran aground on the beach, just this side. I doubt if they could save her now, after the pounding she took in the storm. Captain Lowndes got ashore, along with most of the crew—some of 'em more dead than alive. With the wind blowing so hard, nobody paid any attention to me, so I crawled up over the dune and walked all night to get to Townsend's Inlet."

"So," the captain said with a frown, "that murdering Lowndes is still loose, eh? Even without a ship, he and his gang of scoundrels can do plenty of damage. Those men in the whaleboat told us the Refugees had burned two houses on Peck's Beach the night before."

He considered a moment. "Mr. Gandy," he said, "let's make sail as soon as possible. We'll run up there and see if they're trying to salvage their sloop. Come on, boys— launch the boat and pull!"

Jed got in with the rest, but they refused to let him row. "What you need," said Gandy, "is a good sleep. After that we'll see about puttin' you to work."

Seventeen

THE hole in the schooner's side had been repaired. They sailed her out through Hereford Inlet and cruised north-eastward on a light southerly breeze. Well before dark they were off the spot where the *George* had been wrecked, and Gandy took a boatload of men ashore. From the deck of the *True Patriot*, Jed could see the battered hull of the sloop still lying on its side, half buried in the sand. He had napped for a few hours and felt better.

The Yankee seamen had begun to work at something there on the beach, though he couldn't see what it was. At last, just before dusk, they rowed back. The longboat was low in the water, and as they pulled alongside, Gandy gave a triumphant hail.

"We've got her gun!" he cried. "A good nine-pounder! Rig up a tackle, and we'll hoist her aboard."

The cannon proved to be practically new and made for the British Royal Navy. That night by lantern light the men swabbed out its barrel to remove sand and salt, then mounted the gun forward, where it could serve as a bow chaser. They had even salvaged a dozen nine-pound shot from the wreck of the sloop. For powder they could simply add to the charge they used in the six-pounder broadside guns.

The crew felt pretty cocky as they sailed northward that bright September morning. They bragged about being ready to tackle anything short of a full-sized man-o'-war. But all through the day not a sail was to be seen.

Somewhere off the shore of Barnegat, Captain Hand turned southward again, and all night they beat down the coast in the teeth of a freshening breeze. Jed had been restored to his regular watch now, and he was on deck when the first gray of dawn came over the sea.

"Sail off the port bow!" sang the lookout. "A big 'un! Topsails an' to'gallants!"

Gandy verified the sighting and immediately all hands were called. They were then two or three miles off Absecon Inlet. Captain Hand studied the approaching ship through his glass and ordered the helm put over and the sails trimmed. A close reach to the eastward would take them across the course of the other vessel and give them the weather gauge if it came to a fight. The flag had not been run up.

As she drew nearer, they could see that the larger vessel was full-rigged. She might almost have been taken for a frigate, but there were no gun ports along her side, and her bluff bows had the look of a typical merchantman.

Just after crossing her bows, the *True Patriot* swung over to run before the wind, parallel with the ship. Hand stood on the quarterdeck and hailed her through his trumpet.

"What vessel is that?" he asked. "Show your colors!"

There was a brief hesitation. Then her captain replied that she was the *Susanna,* out of Nassau, with a cargo of Florida beef for the British in New York. At the same time, she hoisted the Union Jack.

At once Hand had the guns manned and broke out the American colors. "Heave to!" he ordered the bigger ship. "I command you to surrender in the name of the Continental Congress!"

To the surprise of the Yankee seamen, the *Susanna* was brought slowly and clumsily into the wind. There was no sign of any intention to make a defense. And Elam Gandy, who had been eager to fire his big new gun, growled in disappointment.

Hand was still somewhat suspicious. He pulled cautiously alongside, with the starboard battery ready to blast her. But the British colors were already fluttering to the deck.

The sea wasn't too rough for boarding, and a dozen men were sent up the ship's side, armed to the teeth. Although Jed stayed aboard the schooner, he had a good view of all that happened. The reason the *Susanna* was so unwarlike soon became apparent. Her captain and mate were the only white men aboard, and her small crew was made up entirely of West Indian Negroes, who had neither the arms nor the desire to fight.

A mournful bellowing and a strong stench came from her half decks, where nearly a hundred cattle were packed closely together. The cargo was far less valuable than some of the other prizes they had taken, but at least the ship was worth something and had cost them no casualties.

With Gandy in command of the *Susanna*, they sailed along the coast to Great Egg Inlet and sent her up river to May's Landing. When the mate returned a few days later, he grumbled over the task.

"Be a month 'fore I get the smell out o' my nose," he said. "An' them pore stringy critters weren't worth more'n the value o' the hides. Five thousand dollars was all we got for the whole passel—ship an' cattle together. Looks like we wasted a week."

Jed could sympathize with his attitude, though he was far from dissatisfied himself. Even after the government took its share, he would get some fifty dollars—another half year off his indenture time.

Those days they had spent in Great Egg Bay had been a period of lovely, calm weather, such as often comes to the South Jersey coast in September. But the day they sailed out again, the wind shifted into the northeast. It was cold, wet, and uncomfortable aboard the schooner. The second day out a big sea broke over the deck and flooded part of the hold, ruining all the hardtack and some of the gunpowder.

Captain Hand headed for the Delaware and home. He knew the northeaster might continue for days, and the vessel was in no shape for combat, even if other ships should be encountered. Like most of the crew, Jed was glad to see the voyage end. He had served in a privateer and struck his blow for liberty.

The *True Patriot* made her slow way up Dennis Creek, anchoring when the tide was against her, being towed by the longboat or by men on the bank when the current flowed upstream. It took two whole days to get her up to the landing and moor her to the dock.

There was news waiting for them in the village. Word had come the day before that Captain Lowndes and his renegades were killing cattle and burning buildings in the northern part of the county. They had stolen two fishing boats near where their sloop was wrecked and used them to raid several homes at Beesley's Point and up the Tuckahoe River. A whole militia company was marching overland to try to catch the marauders.

It was nearly six o'clock and beginning to grow dark when Jed set out for home. His head wound was healing nicely, and he no longer wore a bandage. He carried his belongings in a sea bag. As he trudged past the Corsons' house in South Dennis, there was a light in the kitchen, and he could imagine them all sitting down to supper. If he were to knock at the door, he knew they would be glad to feed him. It was a tempting idea, but he resisted and pushed on. If he hurried, he could reach the Townsend farm in an hour.

Along the familiar trail through the forest he listened for the sounds of animals stirring, but they were drowned by the *shush-shush* of the pine boughs overhead. The northeaster had blown itself out, but a wind still tossed

the branches, and the night promised to be cold. Once a
deer crossed the path not ten yards ahead of him. It must
have caught his scent at the last moment, for before he
could tell whether it was a buck or a doe, it sailed off into
the woods in a magnificent leap.

"Good," Jed told himself. "A few frosts and the venison'll be prime. I'll come over here with a gun and get me
a deer. Ought to be some wild turkeys, too, just south of
here in the beech woods. Roast turkey would taste mighty
fine with some of Aunt Hitty's oyster stuffing!"

With such comfortable thoughts, he covered the four
miles quickly. Then, just as he looked ahead for the first
glimpse of the house, he saw a sudden red glare in the sky
above the trees. Something was afire!

At top speed Jed raced the last few hundred yards.
What met his eyes as he came out of the woods was enough
to sicken him. The barn, filled with hay and unthreshed
oats, was blazing fiercely. In the flickering glow he could
see old Shadrach limping frantically about, trying to get
the stock out before they burned to death.

Jed dropped his bundle and rushed to help. The cows
and calves, he saw, were already out, bellowing fearfully
and tearing around the yard in terror. At the open barn
door, he paused to fill his lungs with air before he plunged
into the smoke. Shadrach was there, coughing and trying
to pull old Brownie from her stall. He caught a glimpse of
her wild eyes as she reared and screamed.

Something Jed had heard came back to him. The only
way to lead a horse out of a fire was to blindfold it. He
seized an old burlap bag off the grain chest and reached up
to tie it over the mare's head. Then he grabbed the halter
rope and backed her out of her stall. Unable to see the
flames, she came after him, trembling but obedient. There
was no sign of Jezebel, the big gray, and he hoped Squire
Townsend had ridden her somewhere. As soon as Brownie
was safely tied to a post outside, he ran back to look for

Shadrach. The old Negro had collapsed and was lying on the barn floor.

Gasping in the smoke, Jed caught him under the arms, dragged him out to the well in the yard, and dumped a bucketful of water over him. When Shadrach began to cough and sputter, Jed looked up in time to see sparks falling on the roof of the house.

"Quick, Shad," he panted. "We've got to wet down the roof!"

He got the old man to his feet and started him hauling up water from the well. Meanwhile, he mounted a ladder against the eaves and carried up buckets as fast as Shadrach could fill them. Fortunately, the cedar shakes were damp from the recent rains, and with the help of the wetting he was giving the roof, the sparks smoldered on the shingles without setting them afire.

About that time Aunt Hitty came out to help. She was waddling from the well to the foot of the ladder with a brimming pail in each hand.

"Thank de good Lawd you's home, Jed!" she gasped. "We come nigh to losin' ever'thing, an' Ah was feared po' ol' Shad would kill hisself!"

At that moment two things happened, almost at once. Amos Townsend came galloping up the lane on the gray mare, and the barn roof fell in with a roar and a crash, shooting up a geyser of sparks.

The squire seemed remarkably calm as he clambered down and tethered Jezebel. He stood there a moment, taking in the details of the catastrophe, then walked over to the ladder.

"Thee has done well, Jedediah," he said. "I think the house is safe now. Come down and tell me how it happened."

"I don't know, sir. The barn was afire when I came out of the woods, on my way home. Maybe Shad can tell thee."

The old Negro was pitifully glad to see his employer. "Oh, Mist' Townsen'," he said, "we done de bes' we could. But de hay's all burnt, an' de oats, an' whar we goin' keep de stock?"

"Don't thee feel too bad, Shadrach," said the Quaker. "We can buy more feed and build a new barn. But I'm puzzled about the cause of the fire. Did thee upset a lantern?"

"No, suh. Ah done finish' de milkin' an' was comin' out again to bed down de cattle. Ah seen two men runnin' back into de woods."

"Two men?" Jed broke in. "One big and one little?"

"Dat's right, Marse Jed. How you know?"

"Joe Crutcher and Al Jukes," said the boy. "They're the Refugees that live up in Great Swamp. I'd figured they'd leave this place alone because generally they don't bother Quakers. The time they took me up to their cabin, it was because they knew I was in the raid at West Creek."

"Well," said Amos Townsend, "don't blame thyself for this. We can stand the loss."

*　*　*

It was ten o'clock before they had supper that night. The cows had to be rounded up and penned, and Jed and Shadrach put up a temporary lean-to where they stabled the two mares. Jed was all for keeping an armed watch through the night, but the old gentleman forbade it.

"Thee go to bed and get thy sleep," he said. "I very much doubt if we'll be attacked again."

This proved to be true. But in the morning, when Jed went out to find the sea bag where he had dropped it, he came across something that disturbed him. Tacked to a fencepost was a piece of dirty paper, and scrawled on it were the words: "Townsen owns Shear of Patriot scooner."

He crumpled it up and thrust it deep in his pocket, for he didn't want the old squire to see it. But the words explained why the Townsend barn had been chosen for burning. At least the vengeance wasn't directed solely at himself, as he had thought.

That afternoon he asked permission to go to Dennis Creek. As he told Amos Townsend, he believed the Minute Men should be notified of the raid. The old gentleman gave his consent, and he set off right after the noonday dinner.

As he had expected, Major Joshua Hand and the other officers were still away chasing Loyalists. But his real errand was to Captain Daniel Hand, of the privateer. He found him down at the landing, aboard the *True Patriot*, and gave him an account of the barn burning.

"I figured you'd be concerned," he finished, "when I found this paper nailed to the fence."

He took it from his pocket and smoothed it out. "I didn't show it to the squire," he added. "But I got to wondering if the schooner was safe."

The captain read it with a frown, then nodded. "It's a sensible question," he said. "Nobody's going to steal a ship this big in Dennis Creek. The whole county'd be swarming around long before they could get her to sea. But those Tories must be bitter enough about what we did to their sloop, and they might try to take revenge by burning the schooner. It's been in my mind ever since we tied up here. O' course the crew's all separated an' gone home, but Gandy and I plan to take turns staying aboard for a while."

"Ay, sir," said Jed. "If you should decide to put to sea again, I think most of us would like to sail with you."

Hand chuckled. "Good for you, son," he answered. "After all you've been through, it shows you've got the right spirit."

He shook Jed's hand, and the boy started home again. On the way he stopped at Jonas Hewitt's house and then at the Corsons'. Word of the fire had spread fast, and he found that people in both Dennis Landing and South Dennis were aroused. Amos Townsend was a highly respected man.

"I reckon," said Tom Corson, "you'll be havin' a barn-raisin' soon. Anyhow, the neighbors are talkin' about it. My pa's as good a builder as he is a shipwright, an' I know he'd like to be there."

It was another half hour before Jed could get away, for Tom and Nancy wanted to hear all about his adventures aboard the privateer. When at last he took the woods trail, it was late in the afternoon, and dusk was falling by the time he was a mile from home. The forest was thick there, with oaks and pines crowding close to the path.

Hurrying along, Jed was startled to see a figure appear suddenly in the trail, twenty yards ahead. He stopped and stared, then saw it was his friend Wagamissi. The Indian raised a hand in greeting and approached him silently.

"You got no gun?" he whispered when he had come close. "Plenty bad white men in woods now. Wagamissi count many as fingers on hand." He held up his right hand with the fingers spread. "All stay at cabin in swamp. Make-um fire, burn plenty house. Maybe want kill you."

With this warning he went back into the woods as quietly as he had come. But Jed had a feeling the young brave was still close at hand, keeping watch over him till he reached the farm clearing.

Eighteen

THERE was a neighborly spirit in sparsely settled areas such as Cape May County. The people depended on each other when they were in trouble. And while everyone knew the old squire could well afford to pay for building a new barn, nobody wanted to miss the fun and social excitement of a barn-raising.

The next First Day at Meeting, several Quaker farmers approached Amos Townsend and suggested a date for gathering at his place. At first he demurred, but their friendly concern pleased him, and he agreed to hold the barn-raising on the following Friday, the first day of October, or "Tenth Month," as the Friends called it.

The word spread to other communities, so that more and more men offered to help. As a result that was a busy week at the Townsend homestead.

Jed and Shadrach worked from dawn till dark, hauling away the charred timbers and the piles of ashes left by the burned fodder. Wrought iron nails cost money, so all the debris had to be sifted to save as many of them as could be found. Meanwhile, the squire had hired choppers to cut down some twenty straight-grained white oaks in the woods near the farm, and a friend of his who owned a water-powered sawmill had started delivering pine planks and boards.

On the last day before the raising, Shadrach yoked up the oxen, and he and Jed hauled the oak logs down to the site of the new barn, ready to be hewn into timbers for the frame and sills.

All week Aunt Hitty worked hard in the kitchen in

front of the roaring hearth fire. She baked three big hams and a dozen pies in the Dutch oven, besides countless loaves of bread. By the time the sun rose on Friday, she had been up for hours, roasting beef on the spit and yams in the hot ashes.

Soon after dawn the neighbors began to arrive. Most of the men were of the older generation, since so many of the younger ones were serving in the war. But they were spry enough, and all were experts at the craft of building. They brought their tools with them and went to work at once.

The families came, too—women and children—all bent on enjoying the feast and the fun. Jed saw Nancy Corson struggling with a huge stone crock of cookies she had baked herself and brought over as a help to Aunt Hitty. He ran to take it from her and carried it into the house. It was his first opportunity to talk to her alone since his return from privateering, but both of them found themselves strangely tongue-tied.

There was little time for loitering. Aunt Hitty chased Jed out of the kitchen and kept Nancy there to help her. Outside, activities were in full swing. Two men who were experts with the adze each straddled an oak log and hewed away with quick, accurate strokes. In an astonishingly short time, they had squared their timbers, lining them up entirely by eye.

Nobody had a blueprint to work from, but by instinct and long practice the builders soon had the sills mortised and in place. Then, as fast as the hewn timbers were ready, they set the uprights, braced them at each corner, and added the stringers.

By noon the framing of the barn was finished. The womenfolk, meanwhile, had set up trestle tables and loaded them with food. Some of them had proudly brought their favorite dishes—corn puddings, apple pies, and other delicacies—to add to the vast supply Aunt Hitty had prepared. There was sweet cider for the young people and a keg of ale for the builders, not to mention a jug or two of rum brought over by some of the Dennis Creek men.

To Jed's amazement, all the food disappeared like magic. In less than an hour the tables were bare, and the builders went back to their labor. There was a shrill sound of sawing now, as the plank floor was cut to length and nailed in place, and the siding began to go on. When the sun was touching the treetops in the west, the barn was finished. All that remained to be done was to roof it with the cedar shakes Amos Townsend had ordered split. And that was a job that Jed and Shadrach could do.

The neighbors said their cheerful good-bys and got into their wagons, mounted their horses, or trudged off on foot. For the squire, the affair had been a godsend, and there wasn't one of the helpers who hadn't enjoyed it as much as he.

Before the Corsons left, Nancy came shyly over to Jed. "We wish you'd come to visit us again," she told him. "Even if we don't have school now, you could come eat dinner with us."

"Thanks, Nancy," he said. "I'd sure like to. Maybe I'll be able to get off from work some day next week. You folks were mighty good to me, and I've missed seeing you."

Jed climbed into bed that night tired but happy. After sunset there was a nip in the air now that October had come, and he snuggled under the warm quilts thinking back over the day. The whole barn-raising had been a demonstration of neighborly good will that left him with a warm feeling of gratitude. He was no longer the orphan bound boy from far-off Nantucket but a member of a closely knit community in which he could pull his own weight.

That sense of belonging was still with him the next morning as he did the milking, then set about building

stalls in the new barn. Well before winter he and Shadrach would have snug stabling for all the stock. And by
the time Amos Townsend was able to get hay and feed,
they would have finished shingling the roof as well.

He was hard at work with saw and hammer when the
clop-clop of many hoofs sounded in the yard. Looking out
through the wide door, he saw a troop of twenty militiamen on tired horses, gathered around the watering trough.
Major Joshua Hand got stiffly down from his big bay and
went toward the house.

Lieutenant Swain stayed with the men. He saw Jed
standing in the barn door and waved to him.

"We heard you got burned out," he called. "But I see
you've got a new barn built. Must have had a raisin'."

Jed went out to greet him. "That's right. We had fifty
folks or more here yesterday. Did you catch up with the
Refugees?"

"We were mighty close once or twice, but we never
really got a shot at 'em. That Lowndes is a smart Tory."

Jed moved closer to his stirrup. "I think I know where
to find 'em," he whispered. "You know that Indian—
Wagamissi—that lives in the Great Cedar Swamp? I got it
from him that the whole bunch is holed up with Crutcher
and Jukes. They took me to their cabin once, trying to
hold me for ransom, but I was blindfolded. So all I know
is that it's some place 'way deep in the swamp."

Swain's eyes sparkled. "So!" he said. "I figured it was
some such setup as that. From there they could make raids
in any direction. Does your Injun know how to find the
place?"

"I guess so. But we'd have to find him first, and there's
no telling where he's going to show up."

"Well," said the lieutenant, "I'll tell Major Hand about
it. We've got to get home and rest our horses, but you try
to locate Waga-what's-his-name. If he can guide us to the
hideout, we'll come back an' surprise 'em!"

The major came out at that moment, the spurs on his jackboots clanking. He mounted his horse, barked an order, and they all rode off on the track toward Dennis.

Jed found no opportunity, that day or the next, to go off in search of his Indian friend. He and Shadrach had to work from dawn till dark to complete the stalls that ran along one side of the barn floor. On the third morning the job was done by ten o'clock, and he set off without asking permission.

It was a cold day, overcast and with an east wind blowing. He started into the woods that fringed the swamp, picking his way through the undergrowth. Every little while he stopped and listened, but all he heard was the rustle of wind in the branches. This, he realized, was getting him nowhere. He tried to imitate the hoot of an owl, knowing that Wagamissi would not be fooled. If the young brave heard the cry of a night bird in broad daylight, he might come to investigate.

At last Jed decided to try something else. He might be able to locate Mammy Shanks's cabin, and perhaps she could direct him to the Indian. He thought back to the night she had led him out of the woods. Groggy as he had been, his woodman's instinct had picked out a few landmarks, and now he set out to find them. After half an hour he was pretty well into the swamp, and somehow the trees around him looked familiar. Carefully he moved on, deeper into the cedars and the boggy ground.

There was a thick clump of brush about the trunk of a huge, twisted old cedar that he was sure he remembered. Then he came to a path, very narrow and very faint, leading northward. It could, of course, have been a deer path, but search as he would, he found no tracks. He followed it deeper into the swamp, where the ground underfoot grew wet and spongy and the underbrush was so dense that he could hardly see ten feet in any direction. He was almost ready to turn back when he heard a sound like a muffled yowl just ahead. He stopped and stared. From an overhanging limb, he saw a lithe dark shape drop to the ground, and there for a moment stood a huge black cat, its yellow eyes glaring into his own. It was Satan, the witch-woman's companion.

He pushed on toward the cat. It turned, its tail twitching angrily, and disappeared into the thicket with a single silent leap. But Jed no longer needed Satan to guide him. The trail was wider now and better defined, and within fifty yards it brought him within sight of Mammy Shanks's house.

"What you' come yeah fo', boy?" asked a harsh voice at his elbow, and he jumped in spite of himself. There she stood, as tall and gaunt as he remembered, most of her face covered by a fold of her black cape.

"I—I need your help again," he stammered. "The Refugees are back, robbing and burning, and I want to tell the militia where they're hiding."

"Hm," she said. "Dey burn yo' barn at de squire's, an' yo' got it all built again. But dat don' put back de hay an' de fodder. Now, Ah don' wan' no sojers marchin' roun' in mah part o' de swamp. Fac' is, Ah don' even wanna see 'em. But mebbe de nex' bes' thing is if Ah call dat Injun boy. He show yo' where dey is, Ah reckon."

From the folds of her black gown she took a kind of hammer. It was small, with a stone head, tied securely to a wooden shaft with thongs of hide. The hollow trunk of a dead tree stood a few yards from her cabin, and Jed was surprised to see her go up to it and start tapping with the hammer in quick, steady strokes. Then she paused, threw back her head, and uttered a sharp, raucous cry before she resumed the hammering. He had heard such sounds before, and it came to him that she was giving a perfect imitation of the largest of all woodpeckers—the bird that irreverent settlers called the "God-A'mighty."

He had no idea how far the sound would carry, but the

drumming beat of the hammer on the hollow trunk would certainly be heard a long way off. After a minute or two the lanky Negress stopped, gave the woodpecker's scream once more, then sat down calmly on her doorstep.

"Yo' may's well set," she told Jed. "He be 'long by-m-by."

Jed squatted on the ground in front of the cabin, noticing as he did so that Mammy Shanks had actually cultivated a little patch of fine green grass there. At that time few homes in Cape May County could boast a real lawn, but hers was as soft and even as a carpet.

They must have sat there in silence for half an hour. There were many questions Jed would have liked to ask the witch-woman, but he kept them to himself. At last she rose from the step and pointed across the tiny glade, and as he turned, Jed saw Wagamissi standing there.

The Indian exchanged a glance with the tall black woman, then stepped forward, raising his hand in greeting to Jed.

"You call for Wagamissi?" he said.

"Ay," the boy replied. "You know the men who burned our barn. Now the soldiers want to catch them. Can you show me how to find their place?"

The young brave's face was expressionless as he considered.

"Me show 'em to you," he said at last. "But no want see men die. Mebbe soldiers catch 'em, take 'em 'way?"

Jed nodded. "Maybe," he told him. "Anyhow, you don't have to be there to see it. All we want is to know how to get to the place."

Again Wagamissi took time to think it over. Then he went to a patch of clean sand, picked up a stick, and began to draw a crude map. First he indicated the spot where they now stood. Next he took his bearings by the sun and started drawing a line northeastward, leading some distance farther into the swamp. Across it he made a wiggly line.

"Small water run here," he said. "Go this way. By-m-by run into Tuckahoe, big water."

"Ay," said Jed eagerly. "That'd be Cedar Swamp Creek."

The Indian drew the continuing course of the stream northward, putting in the most prominent bends. In the curve of one of these, just east of the creek, he stabbed his stick sharply into the sand.

"Here," he said. "This bad men's house."

Jed knelt beside the map, studying it, memorizing each detail. He estimated the distance from the witch-woman's cabin would be about two miles. During his escape from the kidnapers, it had seemed much farther, but then he had been weak and confused.

He rose and held out his hand to Wagamissi. "Thank you," he said. "And thank you, Mammy Shanks. I hope we can catch that gang of cutthroats pretty soon. Tomorrow I'll go over to Dennis Landing and talk to Major Hand, if I'm allowed."

Nineteen

THAT night Jed spoke to Amos Townsend about alerting the Minute Men to the Tories' whereabouts. He had drawn a map on paper from memory, copying the one Wagamissi had made, and he showed it to the old squire.

"That may well be the place they're hiding," said Amos Townsend with a nod. "It's so deep in the Great Swamp few people would ever find it. But it's within five or six miles of all the places that have been burned. I agree thee should see Major Hand in the morning. Thee can ride old Brownie to save time. I'm hoping the shakes will be delivered sometime tomorrow so thee can start shingling the barn."

Jed rose early to finish the chores and prepare for the trip. He took his fowling piece with him. A rifle would have been more useful in case of trouble, but there was no rifle on the farm.

Old Brownie roused herself to a clumsy trot, and they started westward on the forest trail. It was a fine autumn morning and the air felt crisp and bracing. The birches were turning yellow now, and the gums and sumacs were reddening. Frost would not be far away.

Jed thought about shooting a deer. He could do it with the shotgun if he could come close enough and used solid ounce ball. That fine deer he had seen in the half dark, the night of the fire—how he wished he could get it in his sights!

At that instant a bush stirred at the right of the path, and Jed pulled back hard on the reins. The instinctive action may have saved his life, for a shot rang out, and a

bullet plowed into the mare's fat neck. The poor beast screamed and plunged, and Jed was thrown out of the saddle. He landed on his back, still clutching the gun, and rolled out from under the mare's hoofs. Then as he scrambled for cover, he heard a gasping cry. It came from the thicket on the opposite side of the trail—the very spot from which the shot had come.

Jed crouched and remained motionless, his gun held at the ready. The wounded mare had turned and was headed homeward at a stumbling gallop. The tension mounted as Jed waited. He wondered if his assailant was reloading to fire again. Yet the sound of that cry was still in his ears, and there had been something final about it. After endless seconds he stood slowly erect, prepared to shoot at the first sign of any movement.

Nothing happened. Jed advanced, a step at a time, and now he became aware of a still-smoking horse pistol lying at the edge of the path under a bush. Near it he saw an outstretched hand, very quiet, the fingers clutching at the ground. Shakily he came nearer, pushing the branches aside with his gun barrel, and what he saw then made his heart skip a beat. Lying there, face down, was a smallish man in a linsey-woolsey hunting shirt. From the back of the shirt protruded the feathered shaft of an arrow.

Jed pulled himself together, and still shivering, he turned the body over. It was the rat-faced Refugee, Al Jukes, and the arrow that had pierced his heart was of Indian design. Only Wagamissi could have made it and sent it to its mark.

Jed swept the nearby forest with searching eyes, but there was no sign of the young Kechemeche. Knowing his habits, Jed was not surprised. The Indian could appear and disappear as silently as a wolf.

He paused then to steady his nerves and decide what he must do. Jukes might have had companions about, but if so, they would surely have come to the scene by this time.

Nevertheless, Jed looked to the priming of his gun and kept it ready for action. He picked up the big pistol that had come so near killing him. It might be the same weapon that had slain the courier, Jeremy Budd, he thought. Thrusting the long barrel through his belt, he set off westward again, this time on foot.

He had a good deal to think about on that trip. Had his murder been planned simply because he was a member of the *True Patriot* crew? Or had the Refugees somehow discovered what his present errand was? Would poor old Brownie make it back to the farm alive? And if so, what would Amos Townsend think? The sooner he returned and explained, the better. Yet he knew that getting word to Major Hand was now doubly important.

By dint of fast walking, he was at Dennis Landing in less than an hour, and he went to the tavern at once. The major was there, talking to Swain and two other officers, and they gave him their full attention as soon as they heard what had happened.

"The Indian, Wagamissi, drew me a map," he said. "I made a copy, and here it is. If we could get some men together, I think you might surprise Lowndes and his crew. And it would be best in daylight, because I expect they go off on their raids at night."

"What about this fellow who tried to shoot you?" asked Lieutenant Swain. "You say you knew him?"

"Ay," said Jed. "It was Al Jukes, right enough. But maybe you'd like to look at him. I didn't search the body, and he might be carrying some kind of written message."

Hand and Swain got their horses and rode westward on the trail, with Jed mounted behind the young lieutenant. The dead man was still lying as he had left him. Hand picked up the body and carried it back to the village across his horse's rump. Then, in the back room of the inn, he search Jukes's pockets. He had a few English shillings, a pocket knife, and a soiled and crumpled paper.

"Look at this!" exclaimed the major, spreading the paper out on the table. "It's a list of names!"

Jed needed only a glance to know what the list meant. At the top were two names—"Capt. D. Hand" and "Amos Towns'd." Those that followed were the principal members of the privateer's crew, starting with the name of Elam Gandy. His own name, he saw, had a line drawn through it, and when he realized why, he shivered.

"Jukes must have reckoned you were good as dead," Swain remarked. "I see there's a mark like a cross beside Squire Townsend's name, too."

"Ay," said Hand. "That was put there after they set the barn afire, I'll wager. But we've got to get word to all the *True Patriot* men as quick as we can. There'll be more ambushes, more than likely."

He turned to Jed. "That young Indian," he said, "must be a pretty good friend of yours."

The boy swallowed hard. "He save my life," he answered simply.

* * *

Captain Daniel Hand was at his home when they showed him the list of names, and he immediately doubled the guard aboard the schooner. As for himself, he was inclined to discount any danger. However, his cousin, the major, persuaded him to carry a loaded pistol. And he promised to send word to Gandy and the others to be on the watch for Refugees.

"What I'd like to do," he told the major, "is catch 'em all together some place. If Lowndes is with 'em, we could break the back o' the Loyalists in this part o' Jersey, all in one blow."

"Right," agreed Major Hand. "We know where they are, but we need more men than I can get together. What about your crew?"

The captain took a few seconds to think. "I could find

half a dozen," he estimated. "More if we wait till tomorrow."

"No," said the major firmly. "If we strike, it ought to be at once. There may be spies about who would warn them. Get your men armed and meet us on the woods trail east of South Dennis. Let's say not later than two o'clock."

He turned to Swain and told him to collect such members of his troop of Minute Men as he could find and enough extra horses for the sailors. Jed went to the Hewitt house to see his friend Jonas. It was now nearly noon, and of course he was invited to eat dinner with the family. He told them about his narrow escape that morning but said nothing about the projected attack on the Refugee stronghold. It was fairly certain, he thought, that the skipper would pick other men than Jonas for the dangerous job, and the less talk there was, the better.

Jed thanked the Hewitts and walked back to the tavern. Men were gathering there, but there was nothing about their movements that might arouse suspicion. He saw them mount their horses, say good-by to each other, and ride off slowly, one by one.

Inside, he found the two Hand cousins, as well as Gandy and Swain. The mate winked at him and strolled over as if to greet an old privateer comrade.

"There's two horses for us in the stable," he said in a low voice. "Meet me there in ten minutes."

Jed sat down on a bench in front of the inn and tried to look as indolent as possible. He had been lolling there for perhaps five minutes when the obnoxious Zeke Mulloy came by. With the shipbuilding over for the year, he was out of a job.

"Hi, Quaker!" He grinned with a half sneer. "Nothin' to do but loaf now the schooner's tied up?"

"That's about all," Jed agreed. "Not much work on the farm these days. But I guess you know all about loafing."

It was unfortunate that he made that last remark, and

he regretted it almost as soon as it was out of his mouth. He had hoped Zeke would move on, but now he bristled and stepped closer.

"I ain't a loafer," he growled. "I done my work in the shipyard, an' if I didn't have a weakness in the lungs, I'd be in the army now." He coughed once or twice to prove his point.

"But," he added truculently, "I'm still good enough to lick you any day o' the week!"

Jed stood up. "I'll let you prove it some other time," he said. "Right now there's somebody I have to see." And he walked calmly away toward the rear of the tavern.

"Yah!" called Mulloy. "I knew you was yaller!" Luckily, however, he made no attempt to follow, and Jed was soon by himself in the inn stable. He waited there uneasily. If Mulloy or some other observer suspected the Minute Men were gathering and talked about it, a Tory spy might get word to the gang in the swamp.

Shortly, he was relieved to see Elam Gandy sauntering out at his rolling sailor's gait. The mate whistled a sea chantey and appeared to be on no errand of special importance. As he passed Jed, he spoke under his breath.

"I'll ride out first," he whispered. "Follow along a couple o' minutes later, but don't act like you was in any hurry. I'll wait in the woods off the trail."

There were two saddle horses there, and Gandy rode out on the bigger one. Jed's mount was a bony little sorrel with a rattail and a mean eye. He waited the suggested time, then climbed aboard, half expecting the nag to buck. The sorrel made no attempt to throw him, however. It trotted down the road meekly enough.

Jed was all the way through South Dennis and entering the woods before he urged his horse to more speed. Then he found out what the sorrel was made of. Off it dashed, head down and bit in its teeth. Jed had all he could do to haul the animal back to a more reasonable pace. Within two or three hundred yards, he had control, though the sorrel still wanted to run.

"Ho, there!" He heard a laughing voice, and looking over his shoulder he saw Gandy and his mount come out of the underbrush. They rode on in company for more than two miles. Then Jed's nag lifted its head and whinnied. The sound was echoed from the nearby woods, and the mate reined in.

"Off there on the port beam," he said. "The rest are waitin' for us in there."

A moment later they had entered the woods and found more than a dozen horses tied to trees. While they were tethering their own, Lieutenant Swain appeared out of the forest and beckoned to them. Jed still had his gun, his powder horn, and shot pouch. Now he saw Elam Gandy take a long-barreled rifle from a sheath on his saddle. Swain was similarly armed.

"We're all here," said the lieutenant quietly. "Ready for you to show us the way."

Jed looked around at the bronzed faces of the assembled men. The largest number were Minute Men—woodsmen and good shots. Others he recognized had sailed with him in the privateer, and he knew their fighting qualities. All were grim and silent, bent only on the business at hand.

Checking his map, he set off through the more open woodland and skirted the swamp for another mile. Then he led them to the left, straight in among the cedar thickets. By now he was familiar with the way to Mammy Shanks's cabin. He took the posse almost within sight of it, but not quite. There was no reason to involve the witch-woman in this expedition. Now he stopped for a breather. He was reasonably sure he could find the Tory hideout, but he wanted to look at the map once more. Then, as he bent above the paper, he heard a faint rustling noise. Looking up, he saw the men staring open-mouthed at something behind him, and he whirled about to see the tall figure of the witch-woman herself a few feet away. She held up a warning hand, and her voice, when she spoke, was barely above a whisper.

"You in good time, boy," she told Jed. "Dey hain' lef' de place all day, 'ceptin' dat Jukes, an' Ah reckon he won' be comin' back."

Her grin as she said this reminded him once more of her uncanny powers. She seemed to know all that had happened.

"Thank you, Mammy," he answered. "We'll be on our way then."

He waved an arm and moved on into the swamp. The sun was directly behind them now, with only about three hours of daylight left. Jed picked his way through the cedar clumps, avoiding bog holes, and kept a general east and northeast direction. At the end of perhaps half an hour, they came to the banks of a swampy stream, flowing left across their course. It was muddy but not very deep, and Jed waded confidently across, holding his gun above his head. The others asked no questions but followed him to the farther bank.

Now he bore to the left, beside the northward flow of the creek. At the end of ten or fifteen minutes, he turned and whispered to Swain, just behind him.

"We must be close now," he said. "Maybe you'd better warn the men to go quiet."

The word was passed back along the line, and Gandy stepped up. "Let me go first," he breathed. "They might have a sentry out, an' I'll know how to handle him."

Remembering the night at the Fox and Hounds, Jed quickly gave way to the mate. He dropped back to the rear of the file, checked the priming of his gun, and hoped fervently that he wouldn't have to use it.

Twenty

THE cabin of Crutcher and Jukes was a little farther than Jed had figured. For another five minutes the attackers moved silently on along the creek bank. Then Gandy motioned them to get down. Jed was some distance to the rear, but peering through the leaves, he could see the mate advancing cautiously. Soon Gandy disappeared. He must be crawling forward on his stomach, Jed thought.

After a minute or two, the broad-shouldered figure rose again and beckoned them on. As each man passed the spot, he looked down on a squirming, bearded Refugee, neatly bound with cord and gagged with his own bandanna handkerchief.

Then Gandy raised a warning hand once more. The cabin must be in sight through the brush ahead. Quietly Jed dropped out of the line. It had occurred to him that the shack and stable backed up to a bend in the creek, and as soon as the attack came, some of the Tory band were sure to try to escape that way. He waded through the stream and went on up the farther bank.

Nobody saw him go. After a hundred yards he reached a clump of cedars opposite the cabin and waited there, his heart beating fast. Voices were coming from the log structure.

"Pass the jug, Mike," someone said thickly. "Wonder where that crazy fool Jukes is. He oughta been back 'fore this."

Another voice answered with a laugh. "Don't you fret about little Al. He's settled with the boy an' gone on some place. The rebel don't live that can outfox Jukes!"

At that moment a bird whistled a song in the woods. Jed recognized the call. It was the spring song of a robin—and this was October. The Yankee leaders must be signaling their men. A few more seconds passed, and there came the crash of a door being broken in.

"Come out with yer hands up!" Gandy roared. "We've got you all covered!"

There were yells of dismay and a shot or two. Then the rifles of the Minute Men opened up. Jed had no more time to follow the progress of the fight, for just then he saw a tall man steal out of the stable lean-to and dart toward the creek. He wore the uniform of the Royal Greens. It was Captain Lowndes himself!

Jed steadied his gun and aimed straight at the Tory's heart. As the man came dripping out of the stream, he was less than ten yards away.

"Halt!" called Jed. "Don't take another step or I'll fire!"

The face that glared back at him was a gentleman's face, proud and handsome, but now twisted in a snarl. It kept on coming nearer, and now there was a pistol in the man's hand. Jed's finger trembled on the trigger, but before he pulled it, something whirred past his head. He saw the Tory leader spin halfway around, clutching at his right arm, then fall to the ground. In his relief and astonishment, Jed stood still for a breathless moment. Then he rushed forward, his gun held ready.

There was no need to shoot. Lowndes lay groaning and helpless, with the blade of a tomahawk buried in the muscle of his shoulder, Hastily Jed looked around, but nothing moved in the dark depths of the swamp behind him. Once more he knew Wagamissi had come to his aid, then vanished before he could thank him.

All he could do now was stand guard over the fallen captain and wait for the outcome of the battle. There was still some sporadic shooting on the other side of the creek,

and he heard yells of triumph from the Cape May County men. Then the rifles were quiet.

"Hey—Jed!" came a shout in Gandy's deep voice. "Where are you, boy?"

"Over here across the creek," he called back. "I've got a wounded prisoner!"

Within half a minute, the mate had waded across. "By thunder!" he roared. "You've caught the biggest Tory o' the lot! But don't tell me you threw that tomahawk!"

"No," Jed admitted. "He had a pistol, and I'd have had to shoot him if he hadn't fallen down with that thing in his shoulder. I reckon it couldn't have been anybody but the Indian, Wagamissi. Did you get all the rest of 'em?"

Elam Gandy nodded but didn't seem very jubilant. "We had to do some shootin'," he said. "There's two dead an' three wounded, countin' Lowndes, here. Two more are prisoners. But we lost an awful good man—old Ephraim Stites. Well, I'd better tie up this hatchet cut, 'fore the cap'n bleeds to death."

* * *

The wounded Tories were bound to the backs of some of their own horses for transport out of the swamp. The other prisoners were marched out on foot by the victorious Yankees, and the rest of their horses, weapons, and a considerable store of Barbados rum were taken as plunder.

Once clear of the swamp and mounted on the horses they had left tied in the woods, the whole party made its triumphant way back to Dennis Landing. It was past sunset when they rode clattering across the bridge, and the smell of wood smoke rose from supper fires in the village.

While most of the fighters went into the tavern to start celebrating, Jed and Elam Gandy took care of stabling the captured horses. One in particular had caught Jed's eye. It was a handsome black, with every evidence of good bloodlines and gentle manners. Halfway up its left hind leg ran a white "stocking," and in the middle of its forehead was a diamond-shaped white star. The moment he saw it, he had been sure it was the horse taken from the slain courier, Jeremy Budd, earlier in the summer.

"What do you figure this black would be worth?" he asked, as he stroked the animal's sleek neck.

"Don't ask me," said Gandy. "I'm a sailorman. But offhand, I'd have to guess at least a hundred dollars gold."

Jed sighed. It was a great deal more money than he had or ever expected to have, for all his prize money had been turned over to Amos Townsend. And anyhow, who ever heard of a bound boy owning a horse?

He left the uproar at the inn behind him and started for home. It would be a long, dark walk, and at the end of it what would the old squire have to say about his escapade? After a while he passed the place where Jukes had ambushed him. He thought of poor Brownie's screams and shuddered. Perhaps he would come upon her body, or what was left of it after the forest animals had eaten their fill. He clutched his gun tighter and strained his ears to catch any unusual sound in the night that might indicate the presence of a wolf or a panther.

It must have been close to ten o'clock when he came out of the woods at last and saw lights in the farmhouse ahead. That surprised him, for Amos Townsend was frugal in the use of candles, and Shadrach and Aunt Hitty usually went to bed as soon as their work was done.

As he hurried on, he saw that one of the lights came from the new barn. The wide door was open, and he caught a glimpse of dark shapes moving between him and the lantern. Surely none of the Refugees had escaped! But who else could be trespassing at that hour?

Jed approached the door cautiously, ready to shoot if need be. Then he realized that the figures were Shadrach and the old squire. They were working, with liniment and bandages, on the neck of the mare, Brownie.

With a vast feeling of relief, Jed set his gun in a corner and crossed the barn floor. Amos Townsend looked around at him sternly.

"So," he said, "it's thee, is it? And where has thee been all day? This poor beast came home at noon, badly wounded. Was it thy gun that did it—or does thee have some other explanation?"

"Ay, sir," said Jed, subdued by the old Quaker's righteous anger. "It happened in the woods, this side of South Dennis. Al Jukes was lying in wait for me. He fired his pistol and hit the mare. She reared up and threw me, and before he could load again or I could shoot back at him, an Indian arrow killed him. I never saw Wagamissi, but it must have been his. The mare started running back along the trail, so I was left afoot."

He went on to tell the rest of his story as briefly as he could. "The whole pack of Refugees is wiped out," he concluded. "And Captain Lowndes of the Royal Greens is in jail. I came home as soon as we got the prisoners to Dennis Landing."

Amos Townsend's expression had changed from stern disapproval to something quite different.

"Thee seems to have done all I could ask, Jedediah," he said, blowing his nose. "I only trust thee didn't forget thy Quaker principles."

"Well, sir, I kept praying I wouldn't have to use my gun, and the way things turned out, I didn't. Came close to it, though, before Wagamissi threw that tomahawk."

* * *

For a week Jed stayed at home and worked hard at shingling the barn. Shadrach complained of dizziness when he was up on the scaffold, so he busied himself at shocking corn and digging potatoes, leaving the roof to Jed. Old Brownie, meanwhile, was gradually recovering from her injury. At least her appetite was good, and she seemed quite content to stay in her stall while Jezebel and the oxen did such hauling as was necessary.

Jed rather enjoyed the shingling. He liked to handle the sweet-smelling cedar shakes, and he had a fine view from the top of the barn. By Friday afternoon he had finished one side and was sitting astride the ridgepole when he saw a horseman come trotting out of the woods. As he came closer, Jed recognized Major Joshua Hand of the Minute Men.

"Hi, up there!" the officer shouted jovially. "Is the squire at home?"

"Ay, sir. You'll find him in the house."

"Come on down, then," said Hand. "This concerns you, too."

Mystified, Jed descended the ladder and went to wash his hands at the watering trough. Then he joined Major Hand at the front door.

Aunt Hitty answered their knock, stared a moment at the major's uniform, then made a kind of curtsy and told them to come in.

"Mist' Townsen', he yonder in de study," she said, and Jed led the way to the room where the squire was accustomed to read and keep his accounts.

He rose to greet the major. "And what brings the military to a peaceful Quaker house?" he inquired with a twinkle.

"Good news, I hope," Hand replied, "though there's bad news, too. We've heard of a big British raid on the Mullica River. They sent troops up in galleys to Chestnut Neck, hoping to retake some o' the prizes moored there. But the ships had been moved or scuttled, so they burned all the houses and killed a few folks. Next day they figured to march on Batsto Ironworks. In the woods along the road, the patriots ambushed 'em and turned 'em back. That's all the word we've had so far.

"Now for some better news. We sent a messenger off to

tell the Committee of Safety about our raid on the Tories. He's just back with a letter that ought to interest you and young Starbuck, here. Seems the Committee had posted a reward for the capture of Captain Lowndes after some o' the outrages he'd committed up north o' here. I've talked to Swain and Gandy and some o' the others, and they all say it was Jed Starbuck that took him prisoner. Not only that—the men have voted that Jed should have his pick of the Tory horses we took. And I hear he's already had his eye on a likely black. So, Amos, I reckon there's two hundred dollars' reward and a good horse coming your way!"

The old squire beamed. "I don't often refuse money," he said, "but in this case it belongs to the boy. I'll see he doesn't spend it foolishly."

Major Hand left a few minutes later, and Jed started back to his shingling, but Amos Townsend detained him.

"Jedediah," he said, "it's time we had a talk. With this reward and the money thee got aboard the *True Patriot,* I figure thee's more than paid off thy indenture. As a matter of fact, thee'll have a hundred dollars of thy own and a horse to ride. Has thee thought about where thee'd like to go, now that thee's free?"

Jed was flushed with pleasure. "I—I haven't thought much about it," he answered. "Will thee give me a little time, sir?"

"Of course." The squire chuckled, and Jed went out to the barn. He didn't lay a lot of shingles that afternoon, but he did some real thinking.

It was a crisp blue October day. Off to the eastward, he could see the patient oxen moving across the field under Shadrach's goad. Among the corn shocks lay hundreds of big orange pumpkins, waiting to be made into pies by Aunt Hitty's skillful hands. The woods north of the farm flamed with gold and crimson, and he knew there were enough deer and turkeys there to satisfy any hunter. It was a fertile and abundant land.

He climbed down from his perch in the late afternoon, but instead of going about the chores at once, he made his way to Amos Townsend's study.

"Well," said the old squire, "has thee made up thy mind?"

"I think so, sir," Jed answered with a grin. "If thee'll let me, I'd like to stay right here and help with the farming. Cape May County's home to me now—more like home, I guess, than any other place I know."

The old gentleman pushed back his chair, stood up, and held out his hand. "I'll be proud to have thee, son," he said. "Now doesn't thee think thee'd better go and help Shadrach with the milking?"